OTHER BOOKS BY KATHERINE ANDERSON

Hospital Hill: A Novel
Shadows in the Ward

College of Our Lady of the El

Chicopee, Mass.

Murder
at the
Alma Mater

KATHERINE ANDERSON

To my parents, Susan and Kim who began my love
of stories and made it possible for me to attend the
Elms.

For my husband Bruce for making it possible for me
to put my dreams on paper.

This is a work of fiction.

ISBN 978-1-7342621-8-6

Printed in the United States of America

Otherwords Press
www.otherwordspress.net

1953

The hum of voices drifted up from the floor of the rotunda to the balcony where the seniors milled around, talking and leaning on the rail, comfortable and relaxed in a way the underclassmen tried to emulate but couldn't quite manage. The juniors clustered on the staircase to the left of the doors in what looked to be a rather studied nonchalance, though they still managed to look much more at ease than the sophomores across from them, whose first year it was being on the stairs. The Sisters stood sentry at the great wooden doors that would remain closed until the very last moment. As soon as they were flung open the marble floors would echo with the heel clicks of a mob of first years clothed in anticipation layered under their crisp new blazers.

As master of ceremonies, senior Lillian Hanley stood with the Sisters who wore their full habits, waiting patiently for the clock to strike 7:00. Lillian smoothed first her blazer, then the front of her skirt, before reaching up to straighten the beanie pinned to her auburn curls. Once those doors opened the academic year would begin and the seniors would start their breakneck descent down the final hill of their college careers. It was time.

Sister Mary Joseph uncrossed her arms and nodded. Stepping forward, Lillian leaned heavily on the doors and swung them open into the night. The last breath of summer lingered in the dusk that had set-tled over the main campus gates where a statue of the Blessed Mother stood watch over the first years crowded around her marble base. As the door opened, all sixty voices that hummed outside Berchmans Hall quieted at once and Lillian raised her hands like the pontiff at mass.

"Welcome class of 1957!" Lillian smiled out at the girls clus-tered below the wide stone steps of Berchmans Hall. "Tonight we bring you into a sacred sisterhood, a family of friends who will stand by you and remain with you not just while you're a student here at Elms, but for years to come. Once you cross this threshold, the aca-demic year will officially open, and you will forever be a part of this college."

With that benediction, Lillian stepped aside and the class of 1957 tentatively edged their way into the rotunda where they were greeted by the raucous cheers of the upperclassmen. Father Weldon stood to the side smiling and nodding at each new girl as she entered. Sister Rose William stood to his left, reaching out to shake each lady's hand, then guiding them along by the elbow to avoid a traffic jam. It was a well-honed routine, one that Lillian Hanley was proud to be a part of.

Lillian brought up the rear and slipped behind Father Weldon, making her way up the stairs behind the juniors to the balcony where she joined the rest of the class officers who had begun to sing. As the quiet notes of their class song began to drift over the crowd, the noise died down and the first years craned their necks, turning their faces towards the balcony where Lillian had planted her palms on the stone rail while she sang. As she looked down at them, she remembered being one of those girls-- nervous yet exhilarated, thinking they were ready to take on the world. The seniors swayed as they sang, their arms intertwined. Lillian smiled and slipped her arm from Marjorie Rathburn's, then reached into her pocket. They broke apart and a sud-den shower of green poured over the balcony. The first years reached their hands into the air and grabbed at the little felt discs, unfolding them and running their fingers over the golden "E" emblazoned on the front. The beanies were Lillian's favorite part of Elms Night. They symbolized the bond of sisterhood, a passing of the torch to the incoming class.

With their new beanies pinned to their heads like crowns, the girls tugged on their blazers, grinning at their classmates as the light sparkled through the crowd. When the seniors were finished, the junior girls immediately launched into their own class song and all eyes swiveled to the girls lining the staircase to the left of the entrance. The cool night air swept their voices out and across the front lawn, the twinkling of the stars in the clear black sky tinged the edges of the evening blue.

Lillian kept her post at the rail as the festivities continued, her eyes roving over the crowd, when she saw one of the first years slip quietly out the door. *No one should be leaving*, she thought. *The nerve of these first years*. The girl was probably running off to meet someone, homesick for some young man or something. Lillian took a step back and was absorbed by her classmates as she headed for the back staircase that spit her out nearest the door leading out to the quad where she caught sight of the girl heading for Gaylord Street where a car idled at the curb. She couldn't tell if the girl knew the figure in the driver's seat or not but she seemed as if she was heading straight for it. The engine roared to life and the passenger door stuttered open as the driver leaned across and popped the handle from the inside. Lillian saw the girl hesitate ever so slightly before getting in.

The driver wrenched the car into a three point turn, then headed back towards Springfield Street, gunning the engine at the stop. Lillian was already on the move, heading for the front doors of Berchmans. She wasn't about to let a wild, impulsive first year's lack of judgment ruin her carefully planned event. Hurrying forward, Lillian reached the doors and swung the first one closed just as the car roared around the corner and approached the front gates where it swerved, the front tire hopping the curb and spitting chunks of grass onto the sidewalk. Lillian quickly pulled the other door shut just as the car righted itself and a scream tore through the night. She counted to ten before slipping back down the stairs and around to the side door, then snuck quietly inside, back to her post with her classmates who parted once again to allow the head girl to reclaim her spot at the rail for the remainder of the celebration.

CHAPTER ONE

"Listen Nora. Don't get me wrong, the writing is great, as always. It's just not what we expected for your next book."

Nora listened to her editor as he shuffled papers and cleared his throat, a sign that he was uncomfortable delivering this news that he had likely been sitting on for at least a week since Nora had sent him her manuscript.

"No one wants this stuff right now. Your protagonist is a thirty-year-old woman who still lives with her mother, listens to Nirvana, and sleeps with married men." Eric sighed and Nora pictured him rubbing his eyes, trying to stave off the beginnings of a headache. "Look, you're a mystery writer. Why don't you stick to what you're good at."

After she disconnected the call, Nora chucked her phone in her bag and got out of her car which was carelessly and illegally parked in a student lot. She had known well in advance that Eric would hate every word of that manuscript but it had been such a labor of love and she had felt like it was time. Time to be someone other than Nora Phillips, mystery writer. Sure everyone loved a cozy mystery with a vaguely British feel but she was tired of writing the same pattern over and over again. Her heroine was always the same: cute, spunky Charlie Donahue who was, at heart, a dowdy old woman who drank tea and solved crimes from the comfort of a perfectly upholstered wingback chair while throwing flawless dinner parties for potential suspects. It was all just so...done.

Wrapping her scarf tighter around her neck to keep out the arctic blast that swirled between the buildings of her alma mater, Nora headed for the Maguire Center, her coat buttoned tight and her blond hair tucked up into the warmest winter hat she could find that still looked somewhat feminine. It was such a cliche, signing up for a gym membership just after New Year's but she had just had knee surgery and her doctor had encouraged her to take off a few pounds and get herself in a pool, strengthen the leg so that her knee wouldn't have to be replaced before she was fifty. That's what she got for not taking care of the ice on her driveway when she should have.

A rush of warm, damp air greeted her in the lobby, everything looking much the same as it had when she was last a student at the Elms. Nora wasn't the athletic sort in college, in fact the only reason she ever came to the Maguire Center was because her American Sign Language classes were held in one of the classrooms overlooking the pool. The pool she had only been in twice in the six years she was a student there, but it was certainly cleaner than the one at the fitness club near her house.

"Hi, can I help you?" A tiny brunette with a high ponytail and expensive-looking athletic wear bounced up and down on the balls of her feet as Nora approached the desk.

"I'd like to sign up for a membership please."

"Sure thing. Are you an alum?"

Nora nodded. "I am."

"When did you graduate?"

"I graduated in 2001. Then again in 2007." Yes, I'm old, she thought as she watched the girl's eyebrows go up. "Nora Phillips."

The brunette tapped a few keys then printed out a stack of papers for Nora to fill out. "We just need some basic information to complete your membership and then we can get you started."

Leaning against the counter Nora filled in her address and email, all the basic stuff, then checked off about a hundred different boxes that were essentially assessing whether or not she might drop dead on the elliptical, then handed everything back to the girl.

"Excellent. Now I just need a debit or credit card for the fee." Nora handed over her card, wincing as she thought about the advance that was sitting in her account. The advance that she would probably have to pay back since her editor had basically told her, in so many words, that he couldn't possibly sell the garbage she had given him. She waited while the girl swiped her card, then signed the receipt. In return she got a printed membership card, a list of the hours, and a rundown of what machines were available.

"Would you like a tour?"

"No thanks. I think I know my way around."

The girl cocked her head and gave Nora a look. "Are you sure? Things might have changed since you were here last."

"You mean back when the dinosaurs roamed the earth?" Nora shot back. "I've been here since. I know exactly where everything is in this building. It's one giant square with a pool in the middle." She turned and headed for the door, anxious to get in her car and go home to a bottle of wine and a quiet pity party in front of the television. Feeling slightly bad for snapping at the receptionist, Nora threw a wave over her shoulder but the girl had alreadyturned her back to the door and was checking her phone.

Nora's phone was lighting up with notifications too. It seemed Eric had also sent her an email detailing what the next steps would be. Her publisher still had faith in her ability to produce something that would sell so Eric wasn't going to tell them she had failed. Instead he was going to tell them that she needed more time to finish the manuscript. He said he had used her surgery as an excuse, telling them that she had been so doped up on painkillers that she hadn't been able to write for weeks though that wasn't even close to the truth. Point of fact, she had taken exactly one of those painkillers since her surgery and had nearly vomited so that was that for her. And she had actually taken the entire two weeks of her recovery to put the finishing touches on the manuscript that was now going to end up in the recycling bin on Eric's computer.

Well, thankfully that meant she didn't have to pay back the advance. At least not yet. However, that did mean she had to come up with something good in a quarter of the time it usually took her to write one of her mysteries. The problem was she was just plain out of ideas. There were only so many small town crimes you could come up with that didn't bore you to tears as you were writing them. She knew her target audience lived for these kinds of books but at this point, all the ground had been covered unless she wanted to start working in some blood and guts which was guaranteed to shift her demographic and there was no way Eric wanted that either. Maybe it was just time to call it quits and go back to teaching. The money had been good while it lasted, she had had a good run, but maybe this was just the end of the line.

What a depressing thought that was.

Two days later Nora found herself in the locker room of the Maguire Center getting ready to get into the pool for the first time. For two days she had sat on her couch, knee propped up, ice melting into her pants, staring at a blank document on her laptop. The blinking cursor mocked her as she sat there, glassy-eyed, not an idea in sight. She had nothing; nothing but a raging headache and unending pain in her knee so she finally gave in and headed for the pool. If she couldn't do the thing she was being paid to do, at least she could do the second most important thing and take care of herself. Thankfully it was a weeknight and most of the students were in class so she had the pool to herself save one person doing laps in the far lane. Nora immediately recognized her as one of the few nuns left on campus: Sister Eleanor, her freshman year religion instructor. She was surprised to see the old bird still kicking, no pun intended.

Nora slowly lowered herself into the pool, careful not to put too much weight on her leg or, God forbid, lose her footing on the stairs. She got to the last step and glided slowly into the water, feeling the pull on her knee almost immediately. Pushing herself forward, Nora tried to turn off her mind as she brought her arms over her head and kicked her feet, her knee protesting every inch. She had a running list going in her head of possible crimes, potential characters, perfect settings. This time none of it fit together, nothing sparked inspiration.

"Nora Phillips? Is that you?"

Nora had stopped a minute to rest her knee and had her arms spread out behind her, anchoring her to the side of the pool with her eyes closed so she hadn't seen Sister Eleanor's approach. She opened her eyes and smiled. "Sister. Nice to see you."

"You too. It's good to see you back here. How long has it been?"

Forever it seemed. Twelve years since she'd finished her Masters in education that she had only used for a few years before landing her first book deal. "It's been quite a while, Sister."

"I've read every one of your books by the way," Sister Eleanor said as she toweled off her short, graying hair. "They're wonderful. Though I always wondered when you might write about this place."

"You know Sister, I've thought about that myself but I loved this place. I couldn't imagine twisting it into some sort of murder mystery."

Sister Eleanor thought about it for a minute then nodded. "I suppose you're right. But that doesn't mean we can't still inspire you. You should visit the library one of these days while you're here.

During daylight hours of course. Michael still works there. Runs the place now."

Michael Brown. Nora felt herself smile involuntarily at the memory of Mike sitting next to her in Modern Poetry, doodling song lyrics in the margins of his Norton Anthology. Sister Eleanor had, inexplicably, become quite attached to him. "I'll definitely have to stop in and say hi."

"Yes you should. I'm sure I'll see you plenty if you're going to be spending time in our pool. Get that knee healed will you? Oh don't look so surprised," she laughed, seeing the look of confusion on Nora's face. "I saw you walk in. You're limping ever so slightly."

"Gee Sister, maybe you should have been a detective."

"Well if ever there's a mystery here at the Elms, you can write me in as the quirky nun who solves the crime in between shaping young minds." She threw her arms in the air dramatically, her head back as if she had just swept through the ribbon at a marathon, her towel just barely clinging to her chest.

"It's a deal. Should someone get themselves offed on campus I'll be sure to write you in as the hero." Nora laughed heartily as Sister Eleanor's towel began to slip and she scrambled to grab it before it hit the sodden floor. "Thanks, Sister. I needed that."

"You know, Jacqueline is still teaching detective fiction. You should visit her one of these days too."

Nora lifted a shoulder and made a vague, noncommittal noise in her throat. She didn't exactly have much in the way of inspirational words right now, especially not for Jacqueline's detective fiction class. That was the class that made her fall in love with The Maltese Falcon and The Big Sleep. Then they had read Janet Evanovich's One For the Money and Nora had been introduced to a whole new kind of character, one with a sense of self-deprecating humor. Even though there was more blood and guts in the Stephanie Plum series than Nora would ever want to write, she still really liked Evanovich's interpretation of the female protagonist. That was when Nora had come up with her own unconventional sleuth in Charlotte Donahue. She had thanked Jacqueline in the first book but had never actually reached out to tell her about it, though if Sister Eleanor had read them all, it was guaranteed Jacqueline had too.

"I'll tell her I ran into you. She'd love to have you."

"I don't know…"

"Trust me. She'll be thrilled. It was nice to see you Nora. Don't be a stranger." Before Nora could say anything more, Sister Eleanor turned and headed for the locker room.

Ugh. If she knew Sister Eleanor, and she did, she wasn't going to forget about running into Nora. Nor would she forget to mention it to Jacqueline Hall. Pushing off the wall, Nora swam a few more laps, dragging herself through the water until her knee felt like it was wrapped in rubber bands. She pulled herself up the stairs, literally pulling, hand over hand on the metal rail, until her feet were back on solid ground. Her towel was folded neatly on the bottom bench of the bleachers and she wrapped it around herself before sinking down with a groan, her knee protesting every inch of movement. This definitely called for a painkiller otherwise there was no way she'd be able to sleep.

Nora wasn't very fond of the painkillers they had given her after the surgery. They made her woozy and nauseous, not at all pleasant, and she had a hard time understanding why people took them to get high. Was that what being high felt like? If so, then Nora was certain recreational drug use wasn't for her.

A light snow had started to fall as Nora got into her car and headed home. She dragged her feet carefully across the driveway and up the front stairs, careful not to slip, dreading the even steeper flight of stairs she had to climb to get up to her bedroom later. She opened the front door, her cat Hank waiting patiently for her. "Hey bud," she said, running her fingers over the top of his silky black head. "Are you hungry monster?" Hank wound his way around her ankles, leading her into the kitchen. Nora dropped her bag and unwound her scarf, draping it across the back of a chair. Heading for the back bedroom, Nora reached for a can of cat food then bent to let her dog Lulu out of her crate. "Hey princess. Let's get some chow for everyone."

Both Hank and Lulu, Nora's aging beagle, trotted after her as she carried two cans of food into the kitchen and filled each of their bowls, then set them on the floor. As they ate, Nora dug a bag of ice cubes out of the freezer and a carton of leftover Chinese food from the fridge. Lulu left her dish at the sound of the takeout container opening. "Not gonna happen dog. I'm starving." Lulu was undeterred, sitting at Nora's feet looking hopeful as the microwave hummed.

As she watched her food go around in circles, Nora dragged her hands down her face, pulling at the sides of her mouth, bending her lips into a grimace. *Eric didn't like it*. She knew he wouldn't and yet she had still turned it in. Why had she done that? Clearly she wasn't meant to be anything more than a serial mystery writer. The microwave beeped; she took her food and her bag of ice to the couch where she tucked a pillow under her knee and turned on the television, her laptop jammed in one of the coffee table drawers. She didn't even want to look at it right now, not with Eric's words ringing in her ears. Instead she would drown her sorrows in *Masterpiece Mystery* and pretend everything was fine. That was until she heard her phone ding with another email. Probably Eric telling her he had changed his mind about keeping her idiocy to himself. He had, by now, probably spilled everything to the publisher and she was finished.

That would have been preferable to the message she got instead.

To: Nora.Phillips1028@gmail.com
From: HallJ@elms.edu

Subject: Detec Fic Thurs

Nora-
I'm so glad to hear you're among the living! Eleanor told me you're back on campus and you MUST
come talk to my class. I won't take no for an answer.
My Thursday class meets at 1:15. Meet me for lunch
in the campus center at 12:00.
xx J

Of course she didn't leave any room for Nora to say no. She
supposed she could have come up with something, some kind of
excuse, but Jacqueline would see right through it. Instead Nora added
it to her calendar and sent a quick affirmative reply. With any luck it
wouldn't be quite as embarrassing as she imagined.

Nora parked in the circle outside of Berchmans Hall and pulled her
coat close as she prised open the side door to cut through the warm
building rather than freezing completely while walking outside. As she
came to the rotunda Nora ran smack into what appeared to be a tour
group being led by a very chipper-looking blond in an Elms College
sweatshirt, her hair piled on top of her head in a messy bun that she
likely spent twenty minutes on just to make it look effortless. She was
in the middle of pointing up at the balcony above, giving a sermon
about college tradition. It was good to hear they still did Elms Night.
Nora remembered every single one of them, each year closer to the

balcony.

"The freshmen stand here on the quad while the upperclass-men line the stairs." She pointed at the staircases like a flight attendant pointing out the emergency exits. "The seniors are up on the balcony and they drop beanies on the freshmen, welcoming them to the college."

The parents in the group were nodding, looking rather dazed as the tour guide fired information at them while their kids stared at their cell phones, barely engaged as the tour moved towards the door to the quad, exactly where Nora was heading. The Kathleen Keating Quadrangle. Sister Keating was president when Nora was an undergrad, her favorite nun ever (a fact she would never tell Sister Eleanor), and a major influence on her decision to return to the Elms for grad school. Somehow, despite how quickly she shuffled past the group, Nora ended up holding the door for each and every one of them as they spilled out into the quad. One of the prospective students turned and held up her phone, taking a quick shot of the bell tower, then spun around to take a selfie. The parents had huddled near one of the stone benches that flanked the quad while the profros continued to load up their camera rolls.

Nora let the door close behind her as she tried to decide which way to duck in order to get away from the raging hormones and parental misery. As she decided to break right around the cell phone set, she caught the tour guide sidling up to them and dropping her voice to a conspiratorial whisper. "So the bell tower. Did you guys know that someone died falling out of it?"

Suddenly the phones were at half mast and every set of eyes was on the guide. "Yeah, it happened like forever ago. Her name was Catherine, she was a student in like the 1800s."

Nora snorted. Berchmans hadn't even been built yet but *sure, let's stick with that.*

"She was having an affair with a professor, probably a priest."

The details changed from year to year but the basic story remained the same. Catherine was in love with a man she couldn't have, or shouldn't have.

"Someone found out and she was going to be expelled so she climbed the tower in the middle of the night and just…" She mimed a body falling from a height and hitting the ground below.

It was an urban legend that each class perpetuated. Later, when the parents had left their precious offspring alone for an overnight, the blond would grab her roommates and they would take the prof-ros up to the fourth floor of Berchmans to the rail that overlooked the old library to show them the white marble statue that was supposedly Catherine. She would encourage them to run their fingers over the crack in the statue's polished neck, passing by the now locked door to the bell tower that the upperclassmen would look sideways at as they smiled conspiratorially.

Shaking her head, Nora pushed past and headed for the doors of the campus center where Jacqueline was waiting at a table in the back, a cup of tea in her hand. She waved when she spotted Nora and rose to hug her with one arm.

"Long time no see stranger."

Nora hugged her back. "I can't believe the student tour guides are still telling that clocktower story." Jacqueline laughed as Nora settled into her chair, slinging her bag up onto the table.

"That one is never going to die. Did you want food?"

Shaking her head, Nora unwound her scarf and tied it to her bag. "I'm good." The truth was that she had zero appetite.

"So how's the writing going?"

Of course Jacqueline led with that one. "It's going." Nora didn't know what else to say because as far as she was concerned the book she turned in was one of the best she'd ever written but clearly

Eric didn't agree. "I'm kind of back to square one with my current book." Hence the lack of appetite.

Jacqueline narrowed her eyes as she took a sip of coffee, then leaned back in her chair. "You tried to write something that wasn't a mystery didn't you." She shook her head in mock consternation. "When will writers learn? You can't write what you *want* to write! You have to write what *they* want you to write!" She flung her arms wide as beads of black tea exploded from the lip of the plastic-covered travel cup in her hand, landing on an unsuspecting student sitting at the next table. "Oh sorry, I was trying to make a point. That'll come out in the wash."

Nora watched as the student wiped the droplets off her sleeve, then returned to whatever she had been doing on her cell phone. It was a good thing students had a short attention span. "I honestly thought I could break out of the mold but my editor made it clear that wouldn't be tolerated. The only problem now is I'm completely blocked."

"Sister Eleanor is hoping you'll write about the Elms."

"I know." Nora laughed, shaking her head at Sister Eleanor's sudden obsession. "She suggested the same to me when I ran into her at the pool."

Shrugging, Jacqueline pulled her phone out of her pocket and checked the time. "It's not a bad idea."

"We'll see." Nora certainly didn't want to commit to something she couldn't follow through on. As much as she loved being on campus, it had only been a couple hours and she could hardly expect inspiration to dawn that quickly.

"Here's an idea," Jacqueline said, glancing over at the tour group that was dispersing in the front entrance of the college center. "Why don't you write about Catherine?"

"Ha. Sure." With a snort, Nora turned away from Jacqueline and took in the hive of activity around her. When she turned back to

Jacqueline, she realized she wasn't kidding. "You're not kidding, are you."

Jacqueline stood and pulled on her coat. "We should get going."

"Wait, are you serious? Do you really think I should write about Catherine?"

They gathered their things and Nora followed Jacqueline out of the campus center and back across the quad to Berchmans. Jacqueline had one of the larger classrooms on the second floor, wood-paneled with giant radiators recessed into the walls that hissed and clanked as they struggled to throttle steam into the classroom with its massively ancient windows and equally massively high ceilings. It was a losing battle as the cold crept around the floor like a snake dodging around table legs and human ankles, but that was fine with Nora. She loved the false coziness of old buildings.

"Listen," Jacqueline busied herself prepping for class, turning on the projector and firing up her laptop as Nora squeezed herself into one of the desks. It immediately made Nora feel like a student all over again, the first one to get to class, the first one in her seat and waiting for Jacqueline to start teaching. "You have limited time to pull something together, am I right? You love it here, you could easily immerse yourself in this place and the Catherine legend is like a storyline on a silver platter. All you have to do is write Charlie Donoahue into it."

She was right– everyone says that high school is the best four years of your life but for Nora that had been her undergrad at Elms. She had loved every minute of her college experience and probably knew every corner of every building on campus.

"You can observe for the first ten minutes or so while I get them going."

Nora snapped out of her fog, realizing that Jacqueline was talking to her. "Ok, that's fine."

"And then when we start talking about the structure of the novel, maybe you can jump in."

Nodding, Nora pulled a notebook out of her bag and dropped it on the desk as the first students trickled in, each in various states of underdress, their pajama pants and Adidas slides conjuring up images of the aisles of Walmart as opposed to the halls of academia. Nora would never have been caught dead looking like that in a classroom but clearly she had the sensibilities of an entirely different generation.

"Ok!" Jacqueline clapped her hands together with a smile. "I'm hoping everyone read *One For the Money* because we have a lot to discuss today but first," she turned to me and pointed, "I want to introduce you to a former student of mine turned New York Times bestselling mystery writer Nora Phillips."

To say that her students were underwhelmed would be an exaggeration. They barely glanced in her direction before digging in their bags for their books, most of them pulling out paperbacks with pristine spines. Sitting back in the scarred wooden desk/chair combo that she remembered vividly from her time in Jacqueline's class, Nora watched as her friend coaxed her students into something that vaguely resembled a discussion.

Unlike this rather reticent group, Jacqueline's class had been one of her favorites. By the time she walked into Intro to Detective Fiction Nora had had more than enough of Shakespeare and Chaucer— no offense to her other professors of course, but she was a solidly modern-lit kind of girl. She preferred Plath and Parker to Wordsworth and Blake, though she did go in for the Victorian masters of mystery and suspense. She turned her attention back to Jacqueline as every student around her simultaneously glazed over.

"After all, where would modern detective fiction be without Sherlock Holmes?" Jacqueline looked out at her students then glanced at her watch, looking moderately annoyed as she made eye contact with Nora who rolled hers dramatically while the class remained stone-faced and silent. "Ok, you're dismissed. Make sure you check your syllabus for the readings and I'll see you Thursday!"

Nora stood and stretched, hitching her bag onto her shoulder as the classroom emptied out. Jacqueline was still at the front of the room, erasing the whiteboard and powering down her laptop, a few students milling around in the hallway. Making her way slowly in Jacqueline's direction, Nora suddenly realized she hadn't said a word the entire time even though that was the main purpose of her being there. No wonder Jacqueline looked so annoyed. On her way to the front of the room, Nora was stopped by a petite brunette who had been sitting front and center for the entire class period. She was also the only one, Nora noticed, who was taking notes and appeared to have actually done the reading for class.

"Miss Phillips?" Nora looked down and realized the girl was holding not the Janet Evanovich from class, but a copy of one of Nora's earlier books. "I'm so sorry to bother you but I'm a huge fan." The girl opened the book and held it out with a pen tucked into the binding. "Could you sign this for me?"

It was a dog-eared copy of *Nothing to It*, her third Charlotte "Charlie" Donohue novel and one of the best sellers in the series. It was set in an old mill building turned into apartments where an elderly tenant is murdered, her first edition copy of *The Hound of the Baskervilles* stolen.

"This book is my favorite in the series," the girl smiled shyly.

Nora returned her smile. "Mine too." She scribbled her name on the title page and handed it back. "Thanks for reading," she said with a nod, stepping around the girl and heading for Jacqueline who was now packed up and standing by the door waiting.

"Actually..." Nora cringed. Of course there was more. She turned and the girl took a deep breath before blurting out, "I had something I wanted to talk to you about."

Once she was a published author it became de rigueur for aspiring authors to pitch her their works in progress or to present her with a potential storyline in hopes that Nora might use it in her next book. In the beginning, Nora was happy to encourage other new writers but she had learned very quickly that they didn't want just encouragement, they wanted a leg up. They wanted to use Nora to advance their own work which, if she was honest, wasn't generally very good. The good writers knew better than to try to use another, more established writer to further their careers.

Nora decided to head this one off at the pass. "Hopefully not that horrible Catherine legend." She laughed, a short, warm sound that hopefully took the edge off her statement. The girl looked puzzled but Nora pushed on. "I saw you out on the quad earlier when the tour guide was spinning her yarns, taking notes. Honestly, it's nothing more than a story concocted by bored upperclassmen to frighten the freshmen."

Jacqueline was watching them curiously, following the exchange with a smirk.

"There's more to it than that," the girl said quietly. "Nevermind. Sorry I bothered you." She ducked her head and pushed past both Nora and her professor.

Nora joined Jacqueline and they headed for the stairs. "Selena is a little intense," Jacqueline explained. "She's got a heavy addiction to Victorian ghost stories and bleak, foggy mysteries. She's convinced the Catherine legend has merit."

"I can see that," Nora laughed.

"She's also convinced the campus administration is hiding some sort of evidence to do with the real Catherine's death. She talks about it ad nauseam, throwing around conspiracy theories about the church covering up a murder. It's all nonsense." Jacqueline paused, her lips twitching and pulling into a smile that Nora definitely didn't like. "That said, maybe you should talk to her. Bizarre as she is, she might give you some ideas."

The rotunda of Berchmans was quiet, a few students tucked away in corners reading or working on their laptops. Everyone else seemed to have dispersed to their late afternoon classes, back to the dorms, or out to the athletic fields despite the biting cold. Nora never understood athletes and their apparent imperviousness to the cold. She spied Selena with her feet tucked under her in a massive armchair that was nestled into a corner of the rotunda, away from the other chairs that were clustered around a table littered with takeout coffee cups and discarded pieces of looseleaf paper.

Selena pretended to be engrossed in a book, barely glancing up as Nora and Jacqueline passed her. An icy breeze wrapped itself around the two women as they stepped out of Berchmans and headed for the campus center. "I remember the first time I heard that Catherine story. It was when I did my prospective student overnight. Our hostess brought us up to the fourth floor and showed us that statue with the cracked neck. Even I was intrigued by it but there's no substance to it and certainly no crime being covered up anywhere on this campus. And yet, people have been trying to prove Catherine's existence for decades. Without any luck I might add."

"And of course, you and I are rational adults who are well aware that she doesn't exist." Jacqueline opened the door to the campus center and gestured for Nora to hurry in as another blast of frigid air whipped her scarf over her shoulder. "But that doesn't mean you can't use the tall tale to your advantage. Urban legends spark a kind of hysteria, a desperate longing to believe regardless of all evidence to the contrary. I think that makes for a great mystery don't you?" Jacqueline headed towards the college center. "Tea?"

Nora glanced at her watch and realized she had wasted nearly the entire day on campus. "Actually, I should get home."

"Going to try to beat that writer's block?" Jacqueline reached out and patted Nora's shoulder, a mix of pity and amusement dancing in her eyes. "I wouldn't trade places with you if you paid me. Keep me posted. And feel free to sit in on my class anytime you want. Might help dismantle that block." Jacqueline started to walk away, then turned back to address Nora. "I would think seriously about the Catherine thing. It would solve a lot of your problems."

Adjusting her scarf, Nora laughed at the thought of finding inspiration in that ridiculous tale. But it didn't mean she couldn't spend some time reliving her college glory days. "You know, I did write prolifically while I was here. None of it was good but at least I was writing. I don't think I want to write the Catherine thing but maybe just being here will be inspiration enough to get me back on track."

"Don't be so hard on yourself. It's not like you haven't been writing. You just didn't write what your publisher wanted."

Nora shrugged. "Good point. Maybe I'll take you up on another visit."

"Any time. My door is always open. So's my inbox if you need a second set of eyes on anything."

"Thanks. I appreciate it."

Nora headed back into Berchmans and crossed the rotunda where Selena's corner chair was now unoccupied, and out into the early winter dusk where her car was still parked in the circle, little spikes of ice forming on the windshield. Hers was the only car outside and as she opened the door, she looked up at the bell tower that was shrouded in lengthening shadows. In this light it was easy to see why some of the students were so enamored of the legend. She wondered if maybe it was time to give the story some real legs and use it as fodder for another Charlie Donahue mystery. "Oh god no," she laughed aloud. No matter what Jacqueline said, it was a terrible idea.

CHAPTER TWO

When writer's block struck, Nora typically preferred to escape into someone else's writing and steer clear of her own work in progress. Using her knee as an excuse to avoid the world, she hunkered down on the couch and blew through a tower of cozy mysteries while daytime television murmured in the background. Nora locked herself inside the house with a snoring Lulu curled up at her feet, procrastinating with all her might, ignoring her inbox as the new messages piled up.

Eric had of course emailed her with a not-so-subtle reminder that she had a limited window of time to get herself together and hand in a new manuscript, and Jacquline had sent her a few documents, presumably about the Catherine legend. She deleted each of the messages after reading only the subject line because of course she knew there was a ticking clock on her career and thinking about the Catherine nonsense wasn't going to move her forward.

Her current contract was for one book a year, and for five years that hadn't been a problem. Writing Charlie Donohue came easy to her– generally. And it wasn't that she was tired of writing the series; she had just run out of energy for crafting these little mysteries for Charlie to solve. There were only so many ways to kill off the towns-folk in her imaginary hamlet with its immaculate town green and busybody neighbors.

Of course she understood the desire for a series to continue as long as possible. As a reader it's easy to fall in love with characters and want them to return time and time again. But as an author Nora was feeling the pull for something new and different– new characters, new settings. Situations that didn't involve poisoned apple pies and Scooby Doo-style ghosts that turned out to be hoaxes. As much as she enjoyed writing the Charlie Donahue books, the manuscript she had given Eric this time was something Nora was exceptionally proud of. It was something deeper with a different kind of protagonist, someone with meat on her bones and real problems in her life. But Eric was probably right-- her readers didn't want real life. They wanted idyllic stories with no loose ends where the killer never goes free and no mystery goes unsolved.

Sighing, Nora slid her leg off the couch, dislodging the sandwich bags full of ice that were now mostly water. She gathered them up and went out to the kitchen to stuff them back in the freezer where she traded them for a frozen chicken pot pie. Even though she loved to cook, she was in no shape to be standing in front of the counter chopping garlic and seasoning vegetables, so instead she used the toaster oven to heat up the pie, made herself another cup of tea, and sat at the kitchen table to drink it while waiting for her meager meal.

As the minutes ticked by on the oven timer, Nora thought of Selena. She suddenly felt bad for laughing at the girl who had seemed so serious and earnest in her approach. Then she realized she felt something else. Something akin to jealousy. She was envious of Selena's ability to imagine that the Elms campus might be shrouded in some very real mystery. It wasn't like Nora hadn't indulged in similar fantasies when she was at Elms. Nora had done overnight visits at Smith and Mount Holyoke but they were much too big for her, neither did they have the same feel as the Elms. The minute she stepped onto campus and into O'Leary Hall it had just felt right.

As a freshman Nora had been subject to the cruelty of the roommate lottery and it wasn't that there was anything wrong with the friendly blonde she had been paired with; it was just that Nora was looking for something entirely different from her college experience. She wanted heavy wood furniture and an air of gravitas. Instead, Rose William Hall, the first-year dorm, was a terrible example of brutal mid-century industrial architecture with rollaway beds and cheap veneer. She requested a transfer to O'Leary Hall, the girls-only upper-classman sanctuary.

Nora's new room was on the third floor under an eave and she was now rooming with one of her closest new college friends, Margaret. They tucked their narrow wooden beds into a corner near the only window and shoved the ancient wardrobes against the opposite wall, their desks side by side in the middle. They felt transported, as if time had somehow reversed itself and carried them back to the golden age of academia. They reveled in taking the elevator in Berchmans even if it was only one floor in either direction. It resembled the one in *Titanic* (it was a very popular movie at the time) with the accordion-style gate and sliding doors. A relic from a very different time.

Sometimes she and Margaret saw themselves as from a different time too. They wore high-waisted slacks and tweed jackets to class. They smoked cigarettes and carried around dog-eared copies of Sylvia Plath's poetry and Kurt Vonnegut's novels. Nora rolled her shoulder-length chestnut hair back from her face, her high cheekbones dabbed with rouge that made her pale skin nearly translucent. She reached up and touched her hair, now scraped back from her face in a messy ponytail, and realized she hadn't felt that connection to literature, to writing, in a very long time.

A New England college campus in the snow is a sight rivaled by none other. A late season snow storm had shut down classes for two days but sidewalks had been cleared, pathways salted, and classes resumed.

Students were bundled up tight in coats and scarves-- likely the only time they dressed appropriately for the weather- as they dodged snow drifts swirling in the quad. Nora, on the other hand, was wearing next to nothing in her skin-tight bathing suit in the heated pool that felt more like summer on a humid Cape Cod beach than the dregs of winter.

After more laps than she could count Nora was hesitant to get out of the pool and dive back into the deep freeze outside. Then again, it was mid-afternoon and she was starving, plus she wanted to stop in at the library to say hi to Michael. She dragged herself out of the pool just as a group of girls– obviously all members of the swim team- came out of the locker room and headed for the diving platforms at the opposite end.

"That's my cue," Nora muttered, heading for the recently vacated locker rooms where she dried off as much as she could before getting dressed. Thankfully only the bottom of her ponytail was wet so she wound it up into a bun and tucked it under her cashmere hat.

On the other side of campus the Alumnae Library squatted in the crisp, white snow, its floor-to-ceiling windows sparkling in the cold. A gust of heat blew from the open door, a wind tunnel of warmth created by the second set of doors that popped open with a whoosh, then slammed closed again. Inside, the library was as warm as it could be for a 1970s glass behemoth. Normally Nora loved libraries but this one just didn't have the same atmosphere as the ones she was used to. She preferred libraries that lured you into the stacks, encouraged you to hide in the corner with a good book and a contraband cup of tea. This library looked like it kicked you out two minutes before closing so it could have a shot of whiskey before turning off all the lights.

Nora approached the circulation desk. "Excuse me." A young blond looked up from behind the circulation desk. "Hi, I'm looking for Michael Brown?"

The girl nodded and pointed to a glassed-in office to her right, wedged in at the end of the desk.

Nora knocked quickly on the doorway where she could see only the back of a leather chair but Michael's Converse hi-tops were propped up on the heater behind him. "Sir, I'm looking for a copy of the Norton Anthology of Modern Poetry, specifically a copy with inane notes in the margins referencing terrible 90s music?"

"Sorry miss. I had them all confiscated and burned during half-time at a men's soccer game." He spun around in his chair, his hands steepled below his chin and a wicked grin on his face. "Long time no see New York Times Bestselling author Nora Phillips. What brings you to this neck of the woods?"

"You know. Just tossing insults at undergrads and lording my superiority over all our unpublished former classmates." Nora tossed her bag on the chair opposite Michael and swung around the massive oak desk to give him a hug.

"Wait a minute," he said, pushing her away and narrowing his eyes. "You're blocked."

"Oh come on, there's no way you could know that just by look-ing at me!"

He shrugged. "Fine. I saw Jacqueline and she said she ran into you."

"More like Sister Eleanor fed me to her."

"Now that doesn't surprise me." He gestured towards the chair and returned to his, spinning it to face her. "How was it, sitting in Jac-queline's class again?"

Nora lowered herself into the empty chair. "God it was surreal. Not much has changed around here, has it."

"No, it really hasn't. Although they have big plans for a new building. The first one since this fine pile of bricks was slapped togeth-er." He gestured around him at the cold stone flooring and vast expanses of frosted window.

"I hope they get a different architect," Nora laughed.

Michael raised his eyes to the ceiling. "From your lips…"

It would be strange to see a new building spring up on campus for the first time since the 70s. "Where on earth do they plan on shoving it?" Nora pretended to look around for a space, lifting the corners of books on Michael's desk, pretending to consult a map.

"I guess they plan to connect it to Berchmans somehow, right between it and O'Leary." He shrugged. "I find it hard to believe there's enough space for another building there."

"It's going to look like a clown car." Michael laughed as Nora rolled her eyes at her own joke.

Michael sat forward and reached for a bottle of water, took a long swallow, and swiped the back of his hand across his mouth. "So are you going to make your visits to Jacqueline's class a regular thing?"

Sitting back, Nora considered the idea. "I'm not sure. I just observed last time and I'm not sure if I'm good for much else lately." She shrugged. "What do I have to contribute?"

"I'm pretty sure you were doing just fine up until now. You're kind of the queen of the cozy at this point."

"And that's exactly what I don't want to be anymore," she spat, throwing her hands in the air. "If I try to give these kids any kind of advice I'm going to end up going on some post-apocalyptic rant about being a sellout and not being able to break out of the mold, blah, blah, blah."

"Whoa, there killer. Pun intended." Michael held up his hands and pulled a face. "Pump the brakes Agatha Christie."

Nora guffawed. "Even Agatha Christie faked her own disappearance to get out of writing mysteries!"

Michael looked unsure. "I don't think that's quite how that

story went but sure, whatever you need to tell yourself. I think Jacqueline's class could learn a lot from you."

"One of her students is apparently a fan. And a conspiracy nut."

"Oh yeah. Selena. She's in here constantly poring over the yearbooks and taking notes. She's been through every scrap of college history she can find."

"I didn't even realize we had that much to go through."

Typing something into his laptop, Michael spun the screen so Nora could see it and scroll through the list that had populated. "Wow. Dr. Moriarty wrote a history of the college?"

"He did and it's pretty damned good. Might want to check it out just to do it. There's some interesting stuff in there."

Nora considered it, knowing that she was more than capable of falling down a research rabbit hole just to avoid the actual act of writing, and she was well aware that it would be exceptionally detrimental to her relationship with her editor if she got derailed now. "Sure. Sounds fun." Maybe while she was at it she could dig Jacqueline's email out of the trash and read the attachments. "But honestly, the last thing I need right now is a distraction. I'm supposed to be writing."

Michael watched Nora for a moment, a hint of a smile playing at the corners of his mouth. "Jacqueline blind copied me on that email she sent you with all the resources about the Catherine legend."

"Oh come on, not you too?" Nora shot back in her chair and slid down until she was nearly sitting on the floor. "Why does everyone think that's such a grand idea for a book?"

"Because it is. And the source material is all right here in the Glass Palace!" So now Michael was team Catherine too. "It's all still on a cart. Selena's in here asking for it so often that I just never bother putting it away."

"The library is closing soon."

Michael shrugged and pointed to the calendar behind his desk. "Then come back tomorrow. I'm free after lunch."

Nora considered his offer. It wouldn't hurt to just poke around a little. She could appreciate the history of the college without committing to writing about it. Couldn't she?

CHAPTER THREE

Michael had loaded down one of the wooden library tables on the second floor with a pile of yearbooks, folders full of scraps of paper and photographs, and a stack of leather-bound books that dated back to the school's founding. He had guided Nora up the stairs where a cart sat wedged up against the table with even more books stacked on it. Nora pulled a travel mug of tea out of her tote bag and took a sip as she took in the mountain of information Michael had spread out for her. Hiding her cup away, Michael smirked at her.

"You can drink your contraband tea as long as you take notes in pencil." He shook his head and turned away, calling over his shoulder, "Just stack everything back on the cart as you finish with it." He jogged down the stairs to his office where Nora could see him swinging his feet back up on his desk, wondering briefly what exactly he did with himself all day. Nora flipped open the first folder on the pile and pulled out Dr. Moriarty's history of the college. Underneath it were photos of the original dining hall in O'Leary from before the college center was built and another taken from the fourth-floor balcony of Berchmans into the original library that was now the Irish Cultural Center. Absolutely breathtaking.

According to Dr. Moriarty's history, at one time O'Leary Hall was the only building on campus– other than the original chapel- and virtually everything happened inside O'Leary. There was a gym, a dining room, reception rooms, dorms, and a library– all pre-Berchmans Hall and all just so incredibly beautiful. It was amazing to think that the dorm Nora spent three years living in had once encompassed the entire college, that all those girls lived and learned so close to one another. She thought back to the Great Room on the first floor that was only used occasionally for special events and realized that must have been one of the grand reception rooms, one of the parlors. Some of the other photos were more difficult to identify like the refectory-- the dining hall- which looked as if it had been somewhere on the first floor as well judging by the windows. "But where was the library?" she wondered aloud. Had it been in the basement in one of those strange smoky rooms packed with file boxes that Nora had always wondered about?

Flipping over to the yearbooks, Nora dug out a copy of "El Recuerdo", the original title and the first yearbook printed after the completion of O'Leary Hall. There were numerous references to St. Joseph's Hall and the original academy that hadn't yet grown into Our Lady of the Elms.

"Find anything interesting?"

Nora jumped a mile at the sound of Michael's voice. "Don't sneak up on me when I'm clearly immersed in important research." Nora grinned and pushed the yearbook away. "Did you know that this place was originally just a house, a boarding school for girls? It even says most of the families who sent their girls here were single-parent households. In the 1890s!"

"I knew this would suck you in." Michael knew her too well; Nora could feel herself getting excited looking at the faces of classes past and finding out all these little tidbits about the college. "Yeah, the Stebbins Place. It was pretty ornate from the photos I've seen."

"There are a few good ones in Dr. Moriarty's history."

"It looks like they did some renovations but kept its original character. It's too bad the house is gone now."

"Wow. It says the house even had a chapel of its own!"

"And a music room apparently."

"It must have been gorgeous." Nora was starting to lose herself in imagining the girls in their third-floor dorm rooms looking out over the mountains, seeing the Summit House on Mount Tom, watching the sun set over the Pioneer Valley. "The city must have been so different." Woods and fields where the parking lots were now, houses and farms where there were now pizza joints and auto shops.

"Agreed. It's strange to think of Chicopee being described as 'quiet and secluded'."

Michael was leaning over Nora's shoulder, leafing through Dr. Moriarty's history, when they realized there was also a student standing over them. The girl cleared her throat and Nora looked up to see Selena, the one from Jacqueline's class, staring at the two of them, her eyes drifting down to the piles of research spread out on the table.

"I'm sorry. I didn't realize someone already had these materials checked out."

Nora opened her mouth to say something snarky about ownership but Michael silenced her with a look. She angled her face away from Selena and rolled her eyes.

"Hi Selena. I hear you and Nora have already met." Michael was really good at the false cheer.

She nodded curtly, probably remembering Nora's less-than-polite reaction after Jacqueline's class. "Yes, we met in Dr. Hall's class."

"I'll be done in a minute," Nora finally said, throwing Selena a half-hearted smile.

The girl nodded and turned on her heel, dropping into a mod-looking metal and leather chair where she could easily keep an eye on Nora and the collection on the table.

"What is her deal?" Nora whispered as Michael bent over once again.

"She's convinced she's going to one day find proof that our little hamlet here was once the site of some nefarious crime."

"By doing what? Tracking down every student in every year-book and asking them if they remember one of their classmates perhaps being murdered?"

He shrugged. "Your guess is as good as mine. All I know is she comes here pretty much twice a week like clockwork and goes through this same collection. What's crazy is she takes notes every time like she's finding all this new and fascinating information in the same folders."

"Wow Michael. Tell me how you really feel."

"She annoys me." He blew out a sigh and shook his head in Selena's direction. "She doesn't even say thank you anymore."

Nora chuckled, then sent Michael away. She would never finish going through everything if he kept standing there, blathering at her. And the longer it took her, the more agitated Selena was going to get and that in turn would start annoying Nora. Michael retreated to his office and slammed the door, not that it mattered since three of four walls were glass, but at least he could pretend to have some privacy from the rest of the world. Nora continued to page through the yearbooks in silence until she saw, from the corner of her eye, Selena stand and slowly make her way over to the table.

"Can I help you Selena?"

"No. But maybe I can help you. What are you looking for?"

"Nothing. I'm just looking."

She snorted.

"What? Do you know something I don't know?" Nora snapped. "Because I'm pretty sure I'm just leafing through the bucolic history of my alma mater."

Selena crossed her arms over her chest. "I'm sure Dr. Hall told you my theory."

Nora decided to play dumb. "And what theory is that exactly?"

"Murder."

"Well, so far I've found no mention of anything like that happening here. What makes you think there's something incriminating in here that someone else wouldn't have already found?"

The girl looked mildly annoyed. She looked down at the table and tapped her index finger on the file folder closest to her. "You seriously think these are the only records on the school's history?"

"It's hearsay Selena. A story you've conjured out of thin air after hearing the same ridiculous urban legend they've been telling for decades, a hazing ritual like streaking across the quad or putting lingerie on the religious statues." Selena blinked. Well, it appeared she had heard *that* story too. To this day the nuns still had no idea that Nora and her roommate Margaret had been responsible for that particular prank. It was amazing what lived on in the student memory and what didn't. "There's absolutely zero merit to that Catherine story."

Selena's cheeks reddened and her mouth pulled tight in a grimace. It appeared Nora had hit a nerve. She lowered her head and smiled. "It's really not just a story. And it's all in there somewhere."

"All what Selena? There's nothing here but the history of the college. If anything like a murder had occurred here, don't you think there would be some record of it?"

"Of course not." Selena shook her head at Nora. "Do you know how powerful the church is?"

Nora sat back in her chair and eyed Selena. "So you're not only a believer in urban legends but you're also a conspiracy theorist? The Catholic Church certainly makes a nice target for that kind of thinking, I'll agree, but I don't think a small Catholic college in the boondocks of Western Massachusetts is high on their radar when it comes to covering up a murder."

"They would if the murderer was a member of the church."

"No one here is important enough to warrant that kind of protection."

"They do it when it's a sex scandal. Why not a murder?"

"Because there was no murder." Nora pushed away from the table and stood up. "It's all yours Selena. Enjoy your wild goose chase." She slid her travel mug back into her bag and slung it over her shoulder, draping her coat over her arm as she moved to leave.

"This isn't all of it," Selena said quietly, so quietly that Nora almost didn't hear her at first.

"All of what?"

"All the history. All the information." Selena looked over her shoulder at Nora as she moved to sit in the chair Nora had just vacated. "There's more."

"Where?" *Damn it*. Nora had walked right into her trap, her curiosity getting the better of her common sense.

"I don't know if I should show you. Since you don't believe me."

Nora sighed. "You should show me. Consider it your one chance to convince me."

With a nod, Selena reached out a practiced hand and swept everything on the table into a neat pile, handing half to Nora to reshelve on the cart. They silently moved down the stairs past Michael's office where Nora caught Michael's look of confusion and tossed a shrug in his general direction. She trailed Selena out into the freezing cold and across the quad to O'Leary where they climbed the stone steps to the front door. Nora waited while Selena swiped her ID card, then stopped at the desk positioned just inside the door to sign her in. "I see things haven't changed much," Nora remarked.

"They never do here. Thank God." So Selena also appreciated nostalgia too. "I'm on the third floor. I just need to drop my stuff."

At the top of the stairs, Selena took a left and headed down the narrow hallway, then around a corner to a room tucked under the eaves. "My goodness it's a small world," Nora laughed as Selena unlocked her door. "This was my room junior year."

"You're kidding?"

"Not in the least. I loved this room because we had this little dead-end hallway all to ourselves." She gestured to the two windows tucked into the hallway alcove with their broad windowsills, just right for sitting on. "We had a snowstorm that shut down the campus one weekend. No power, nothing. My roommate and I sat out here in front of the radiators and read magazines all day."

Selena paused, looking somewhat pained. "I do the same thing. Except I don't have a roommate. She dropped out after the first month and they never assigned me anyone new."

"Be grateful. I will never understand the emphasis put on learning to live with a roommate. All you ever learn is how to hide your food and fight over the remote."

"Sometimes it sucks more being here alone." The inside of Selena's room looked exactly as Nora would have described it if Selena was a character in one of her novels. There were books everywhere, papers on every available surface. She had multiple cork boards hanging on the angled walls and they were covered with what Nora assumed was her research into the college's history.

"This looks like a serial killer board." Nora walked over to the first board and leaned close, recognizing a number of the photos tacked to it, many of them half-covered in Post-It notes crowded with Selena's angular yet girlish handwriting.

"That's essentially what it is," Selena replied, coming to stand next to Nora.

"Do you think there was more than one murder?"

Selena shrugged. "I'll be honest. I'm not entirely sure at this point. First I'd like to just prove there are secrets here."

They stood side by side and stared at the boards together, Nora still finding it hard to believe that this girl was so convinced not only that someone had been murdered at the Elms, but that it might be part of a larger plot deep inside the church that could ostensibly stretch to multiple murders. "I think you're reaching on that one. You'll be hard-pressed to convince me there was one murder, let alone a series. And everyone has secrets, there's nothing new or interesting about that."

She shrugged again. "Well, let me show you what I'm working with."

"Where?" Nora asked again as Selena headed for the door.

"I told you I'd show you the rest of it. Just follow me."

Selena locked the door behind her and headed for the stairs. When she got to the first floor, she looped around the ornate banister and made her way to the dark, narrow flight that continued down to the basement where Nora was greeted with the familiar sound of the ratty old washing machines walking across the tile floor of the cave-like kitchen cum laundry room tucked under the stairs. Also tucked under the stairs was Nora's favorite room in the entire building. She stopped at the foot of the stairs and looked over at the door, unchanged, and remembered the night she and her roommate had discovered it after heating up canned spaghetti and meatballs in the kitchen.

"Where does this door go?" Margaret had asked, peeking under the stairs and finding a green wooden door jammed into the corner. "I never realized there was a door here."

To be fair, the door was rather well hidden by the metal rail on the basement stairs and a tangle of steam pipes that had been painted with bubbles and creepy bits of poetry. "I never noticed it either. It's probably locked." Nora had hoisted herself up on the counter next to the stove so she could watch the pan of spaghetti while also keeping an eye on Margaret who had a habit of getting herself into trouble when left unsupervised. Leaning to the left a little, she could see Margaret reaching out for the door, effortlessly swinging it open.

"It's pitch black in here." Margaret disappeared and Nora could hear her banging around, presumably searching for a light switch. Switching off the burner, Nora slid off the counter and joined Margaret. A moment later the walls were illuminated by a weak, dirty yellow light thrown from aging sconces that likely hadn't been dusted since the 1950s, the era from which the few bits of furniture appeared to be as well.

The walls were wood paneled, solid wood, not that fake stuff that cropped up everywhere in the 1970s. It was smooth to the touch as Nora caught up to Margaret and ran her fingers along the polished planks. The outside wall ran the length of the side of the building, just as in the great room above which Nora realized they were now standing directly below– the space the girls called the "piano room"- and the rooms couldn't have been more opposite. Where the piano room had massive ceilings and soaring windows that threw sunlight across the robin's egg blue walls, this room had a low ceiling that Nora could touch without even rising to her toes. The windows were tiny squares at the top of the outside wall and though it was dark out now, it was obvious that they let in very little light.

The furniture in the piano room was elegant and unoccupied 364 days out of the year while the furniture in the basement room looked comfortable and lived in. The cushions on the emerald green couch were squished down, shaped to generations of bodies that had occupied it over the years. If it wasn't for the coating of dust on the fabric Nora would have assumed someone had just vacated their seat in search of a snack. It made her think of a secret society, very Dead Poets. There was even an enormous slate-topped billiards table in the middle of the room.

The one feature of the room that seemed rather out of place was the fireplace mantle that reached nearly to the ceiling, though that wasn't hard to do when the space was already so dwarfed by being tucked into the foundation. The wood was ornately carved, the hearth tiled neatly and swept clean. The hardwood floors were scuffed and scratched, the mark of so many feet shuffling around the billiards table or perhaps dancing to records on a record player that no longer existed. The only other furniture was a grouping of wooden chairs in the far back corner but otherwise, the room was nearly bare.

"This room is amazing. It doesn't look like anyone has used it in ages." Nora started sweeping dust off the couch cushions, beating the palm of her hand against them and filling the air with swirling motes that floated in the dank pools of light above the wall sconces.

"We should claim it as our own," Margaret had suggested, sticking her hand in one of the nets on the billiards table and pulling out a solid orange ball marred by black smudges from repeated play. "We could come down here any time we want as long as we don't tell anyone about it."

And they hadn't. It became their own private lounge, one they really only frequented after hours when everyone else was either in the college center participating in some sort of group activity or already tucked away in their rooms writing papers and studying. Margaret and Nora spent hours reading on that green couch and playing pool, though some of the balls were missing and there was only one cue that Margaret found tucked behind the mantlepiece.

Unlike Nora and Margaret, Selena breezed down the stairs without even glancing towards that old hideout. Nora imagined that she and Margaret had been the last girls to use that room, a thought that made her smile briefly until she realized that Selena had gotten quite a ways ahead of her. She led Nora to the middle of the basement where a square had been built, clearly as an afterthought, and Nora remembered it as being temporary office space that had then become storage. When she was living in O'Leary back in the late 90s those rooms had all been locked.

Selena walked confidently up to the first door on the left and pulled out her Elms lanyard where Nora could see she had a second key that was much smaller and bore no resemblance to any of the student keys that circulated around campus. Sliding it into the lock, Selena glanced down the hallway as if she expected someone to come out of the shadows and grab the key out of her hand but there was no one there. The entire dorm building was steeped in silence. Stepping back, Selena allowed Nora to go through the door first while she reached in to flip the light switch, bringing to life row after row of fluorescent tube lighting that hung from the ceiling over walls that didn't go all the way up.

File boxes and recycled printer paper boxes were stacked haphazardly on nearly every surface that wasn't crowded with discarded furniture. Nora recognized the small wooden desks that had once decorated every dorm room in the building jumbled together with their accompanying armchairs that bore the Elms College seal, chairs that had been in the dorm rooms for hundreds of years and that Nora remembered sitting in on so many afternoons studying before Margaret got out of class and they could retreat to their basement lair.

"I don't know what the story is behind these rooms but obviously they've become storage. Most of it completely ignored." An avalanche of old receipts had poured out of a broken and slightly damp-looking box, spilling out onto the carpet that was flecked with plaster dust and shards of peeled paint. There had been water damage down here at one point, damage that no one had seen fit to repair it seemed. Nora wondered if perhaps one of the claw foot tubs in the communal bathroom above had overflowed.

"They were here when I was living in O'Leary too. In pretty much the same state. I don't think I ever saw anyone going in or out."

"Everything towards the front is fairly new. Receipts from the bursar's office. Boxes of pamphlets and prospective student packets. Things like that." At the back was a door that connected with the next room and Selena bumped it open with her hip. "It swells a bit and gets stuck." The door scraped along the carpet as it groaned open, the room already lit by the shared fluorescent bulbs that made the rooms appear almost sterile in their decay, the paint hanging in strings from above like so many white spiderwebs that had been pulled down by the wind.

As students, Nora and Margaret had explored these rooms too. Even though all the doors were locked, the walls didn't reach all the way to the ceiling and Margaret discovered she could climb over the top and hop from room to room, Nora following her at a slightly slower pace. Then, as now, Nora marveled at how the paint and plaster on the ceiling appeared to only be peeling within the confines of that square of rooms, despite the fact that it was the same ceiling that hung over the pristine basement hallways as well.

Selena walked over to a table that was far more organized than the rest and leaned against the edge, gesturing to the contents like a game show host revealing the board. "I've taken some of the material upstairs but I didn't think taking it all at once was a good idea."

"You actually think someone would notice it was gone?" Nora leaned over to inspect the girl's handiwork. "They'd be more likely to notice it neatly organized than missing altogether in this rat's nest."

"I tried to organize everything I found, clearly. I'll tear it apart again when I'm done."

"Cover your tracks. Smart. You don't want anyone grabbing your story before you've finished."

It was sarcasm of course but the girl took Nora's comment seriously, nodding thoughtfully before picking up the first pile of papers and handing them to Nora. "This was the first thing I ever found down here."

She handed Nora a newspaper article about the start of classes dated 1953. There was a photograph of the incoming freshman class assembled on the front stairs of Berchmans, all dressed smartly in their blazers with little green beanies perched on their perfectly coiffed hair. The piece took up the entire front page of the *Sunday Republican*, the special weekend issue of the city daily, *The Union News*. Skimming the article, Nora struggled to figure out why this particular piece had grabbed Selena's attention. She looked up at the girl and shrugged.

"Look at the lower right corner."

A tiny line item that anyone could have missed. "College student thought missing after first night celebrations," Nora read aloud. "What student?"

Selena lifted a shoulder. "That's the only item and I haven't been able to find any kind of followup. I even went through the *Republican*'s archives. I found nothing."

"Then I'm guessing whoever she was, she was found rather quickly and the school declined any further attention from the press."

"That's one thought. Or…"

"Or something happened to a student and the school covered it up," Nora supplied with a roll of her eyes and a deep sigh. This kid and her theories.

"I've tracked down most of the class of 1957 who were first years when this article came out, the ones who are still alive anyway. Some of them remembered something of a disturbance at Elms Night but never knew what that was or who was involved. One woman swears she heard a scream. Another said she remembers the head girl from the senior class pulling the doors closed even though it was blazing hot in the rotunda. She thought maybe that had something to do with the girl going missing. Nothing concrete though."

Maybe she was right, this was certainly interesting but not a smoking gun by any means. "What else did you find?"

Sifting through the paperwork Selena drew out another article and handed it to Nora. It was a piece about an art exhibit in the rotunda of Berchmans. But once again, that was not why this particular article had caught Selena's eye. Another line item in the lower corner: *Elms College student dies unexpectedly; illness suspected.*

"There's no follow-up for that one either."

Nora shrugged. "There wouldn't be, I suppose, if they suspected she had been sick. No name again I see."

"Both girls were likely minors. They wouldn't have released their names."

"Oh I know, but it doesn't give you much for leads." Handing the paper back to Selena, Nora paced to the other side of the room and back, her hand on her chin, her index finger scratching absentmindedly at the corner of her mouth. "Ok you've got something rather curious here, I'll give you that. But I don't see any kind of connection between these two stories."

"I'm *certain* they're connected somehow."

Shaking her head, Nora picked up the article about the missing girl again. "At this point, you're reaching. Maybe even overreaching, I'm not sure, but it's a common mistake when you first start looking into something like this. You have to look at what you've got so far and try not to get tunnel vision. You're excited, I can see that, and you want it all to fit together, but you risk missing important information."

"But I know..."

"No, you don't. You assume. You presume. You hope." She waved the article at Selena. "Nothing is certain except that you've found two rather vague and mysterious line items in a newspaper that conjure up a bit of mystery."

"Well, beyond searching the newspaper archives I have no idea where to start," she admitted quietly. For all her bluster and bravado about this, it seemed Selena really didn't know what she was doing. She was just a first year after all, one who was likely living away from home for the first time and desperate to find a story, any story. Nora admired her enthusiasm but that was all she had, her curiosity and her determination.

Nora sighed heavily. "I can help with that. But first, we need to filter through the rest of this. There might be something you missed the first time." Nora put up her hand to stop Selena from protesting the perceived dig. "I'm not saying you're not capable. I'm saying you need a second set of eyes. You stare at the same thing long enough and you go blind to everything else. Trust me. I know."

"Fine. Then let's get started."

"You don't waste any time," Nora laughed.

"Well, clearly I've already wasted plenty of it by developing tunnel vision as you say."

"It's ok. Your drive is admirable." Nora smiled in spite of herself. "You just need direction."

"And you're to be my compass I presume?"

"I have contacts you don't have. I have access to things you wouldn't be granted without a lengthy research proposal. I have…"

"I know. Your name carries weight around here. I get it."

It was true. Being published and having a higher-than-average Google search rating made it easier to open certain doors. "You'll get there. Make something of this and it'll be *your* name opening the doors."

CHAPTER FOUR

Nora sat in her office and dragged Jacqueline's email out of the trash, filtering through the collection of attachments she had sent. One was Dr. Moriarty's history of the college which she had already read but downloaded anyway. The other, an article written for the school newspaper in the late 1930s, talked about the Catherine legend and initial speculation as to the story's origins.

> *Legend has it that Elms College was the site of a grisly*
> *student death. Catherine, a young woman attending the*
> *college, leaped (or was pushed) from the bell tower of*
> *the administration building. The building dates to 1929*
> *but it is unclear how long the legend of this troubled*
> *woman has been whispered from one student to another.*

Clearly, no one had a solid handle on the legend, not even the generations who were supposedly there when it happened. It didn't matter; at this point, Nora was no longer interested in the fairytales, just the facts.

There truly were some great photos in Dr. Moriarty's history, especially the photos of the nuns who had founded the original academy. Nora especially loved the early photos of the chapel that was built around the same time as Berchmans as it was one of her favorite buildings on campus. It would be even better if there were other photographs out there of the college, maybe around the time those line items had been written. She wondered if there were any online, maybe in Digital Commons, or maybe even eBay. Nora had found numerous postcards of the college for sale on the auction site but she had never thought to look for photographs too. Opening her account, she typed in her search but "Elms College" alone returned hundreds of results, most of them resellers with Blazers sports merchandise but when Nora changed her search to College of Our Lady of the Elms, she struck gold.

Amidst the many postcards was a beautiful sepia-toned press photo of the library on the third floor of Berchmans. It must have been taken right after the building was completed and furnished because the shelves were still empty of books and the tables had perfect glassy surfaces. The soaring cathedral windows were absolutely gorgeous. Nora's heart actually skipped a beat looking at that incredible new space that would soon be filled with girls studying and relaxing, reading their favorite books under the glow of the reading lamps that were now considered antiques. She surprised herself by buying the photo, anxious to hold it in her hands, to look at every detail of the room up close.

Nora hated the term "old soul" but she guessed if she had to put herself in a category that would be it. She looked at things like this photo of the library and wished herself in that era. She appreciated antiques, old wood, vintage styling. Her kitchen was filled with Pyrex, her furniture was midcentury. Nora equated that era with coziness, the comfortable feel of a cottage in the woods. It was also a hobby, going to antique shops and flea markets with her mother to pick through yards and yards of other people's junk, sifting through old photographs, hoping they would give her ideas for new characters. To find a mystery that was not only unsolved but also embodied that entire era was a windfall for Nora.

One of the main reasons she had chosen the Elms was because

it felt like the buildings were stuck in another era. There was always an air of mystery and tradition that made it easy for Nora to imagine she was there when the beanies were new and the blazers were crisp, the nuns enforced curfew and the professors arrived in suits and skirts. It was one of the few places where Nora's retro style didn't stick out painfully, drawing disapproving stares from her contemporaries as they had when she was in high school. At college, that kind of creative spirit was encouraged. After all, it was a time of exploration, of finding oneself, and that was what Nora did.

Had those two girls, the ones who had been reduced to a few words in the farthest corner of the paper, had a chance to find themselves? Did they know who they were before they disappeared from campus? Before one of them died under perhaps questionable circumstances? Nora was hoping she might have an opportunity to find out. In the meantime she dug into the notes she had taken from the pile of research Michael had shared with her. She hadn't gotten through much of it before Selena had interrupted but it was enough to narrow her focus. It was 1953 so both girls lived in O'Leary, ate in O'Leary, and socialized in O'Leary. Those makeshift storage rooms only dated back to the early 1990s, so what was there in 1953?

"Does it matter what was there?" Nora asked her computer scream. There had been yearbooks in the pile Michael had shown her but none that dated back far enough which made her wonder what the odds were that perhaps they had been digitized. Best-case scenario would be finding a yearbook for 1953 but at that point, anything from that time period might give Nora a better idea of what life looked like at the time those two girls disappeared. Ancestry.com had a rather extensive collection of yearbooks and Nora whooped with joy when 1953 appeared in the results. As the file loaded, she took a sip of the tea she had brought up with her that was now lukewarm and barely drinkable but she didn't even notice.

Zooming in on the black and white pages, Nora scanned each one carefully, taking in every detail of every photo, even the backgrounds of the formal portraits, but especially the candids. Halfway through the book nothing seemed out of the ordinary, there was nothing that gave Nora pause until she happened on a page filled with candids– photos of events in Veritas Auditorium, easily identified by the rows of burgundy velvet seats and dramatic chandeliers, group photos out on the quad, on the steps of O'Leary, in front of the main gates. But one image in particular caught her eye, what looked like a party with girls in taffeta dresses and booths in silk ties. Though it wasn't the party itself that had jumped out at her.

There, in the center of the festivities, holding a crystal punch bowl, was a piece of furniture that, though it had a tablecloth over it, Nora would know anywhere. Enlarging the image as much as possible, Nora dragged it around her screen, picking out a fuzzy green sofa, a mantle that was clean and polished with an elegant oil painting hanging above. There was no doubt that was the pool table serving as a refreshment stand in the basement lounge that Nora and Margaret had spent so many hours in.

Nora took a screen capture and saved the photo to her desktop, then continued flipping through the yearbook. There was another page of candids ¾ of the way in with another photo of the same party, this one taken from the other end of the room with couples dancing, a record player set up in the corner. From that angle the entire room was visible and Nora wondered if the girl who died was in this picture. "Only one way to find out," Nora muttered to herself, saving the second picture. It was time to ask some questions but first, she owed Jacquline a visit.

CHAPTER FIVE

Once again Nora found herself sitting in Jacqueline's detective fiction class but this time she was there to talk about her process when writing her Charlie Donahue series. She planned to talk a little about the research that went into the books— God help her if anyone ever looked at her internet search history– and how she organized her writing. Which was not at all. A lot of writers talked about how they outlined and plotted and crafted but Nora usually just wrote. She tried being a planner, creating outlines, filling out character questionnaires, but it didn't work for her. Once she got an idea, it just flowed. Sometimes she started at the beginning, sometimes in the middle. A few times she had come up with an ending long before she even built out the characters Charlie would encounter. She scribbled notes on Post Its and stuck them to the wall or pinned up a mess of note cards that she could move around as she maneuvered the plot. For her, it had to be a fluid process.

Some of the students had started to trickle in as Nora was reviewing her notes, Selena striding in at the tail end of a group of girls huddled in their Elms College sweats and Ugg boots. She caught Selena giving the girls a once over with a slight eye roll, realizing that every time she saw Selena she was neatly dressed and fully made up. In fact, now that she was paying closer attention to the girl, she realized she had something of Audrey Hepburn about her with skinny black pedal pushers and neat blouses with elegant collars. Even her coat had an air of sophistication to it that made it look stylish and tasteful in its simplicity. Her long brown hair was pulled up in a high ponytail with a strand wrapped around to hide the elastic. Very old Hollywood.

She had bright blue eyes, a much brighter blue than Nora's whose were closer to blue-gray. While Nora's hair was just as long as Selena's, perhaps a bit longer, hers was darker, nearly black, and she usually wore it in a messy knot on top of her head, pieces constantly flying around her face. Selena, however, was always perfectly coiffed and had the pale, smooth skin that is found only in youth. Like porcelain. Nora had once had skin like that but now she had a sprinkling of freckles across the bridge of her nose and little lines at the corners of her eyes, likely from squinting at a computer screen for hours on end every day. Even wearing her glasses wasn't helping her eyesight these days.

Jacqueline began her class and got everyone settled before calling on Nora to give her presentation. She hadn't prepared slides or anything but had brought along a few of her notebooks and drafts to share. Clearing her throat, she realized she was actually nervous which was funny since she regularly read for much larger groups on her book tours. Now, in front of this group of disinterested college students, she felt her knees quaking and her palms sweating. She looked out at the passive faces and caught Selena's eye as she sat ready, pen to paper. The encouraging look Selena gave Nora galvanized her and she began talking despite the rushing sound in her ears.

"I've been writing since I was a kid. My mother said she could never find pens or paper in our house because I regularly pilfered the tools of my trade." The class emitted a nearly inaudible chuckle, but it was a response nonetheless. "I wrote my first successful story in 4th grade about an abandoned nightclub my parents took me to see. Yes, I recognize that that's a strange thing to show your child but my parents loved history and loved mysteries. They took me to see all kinds of historic and sometimes forgotten places. In a way, that's how Charlie Donahue was born."

Nora went on to talk about creating the character, how she had her roots in Agatha Christie's Marple and Alice Kimberly's haunted bookshop heroine, Penelope Thornton-McClure. She always imagined Charlie as being not of her time, an intellectual with a nose for crime. Suddenly a hand went up in the middle of the Ugg girls.

"Do you make a lot of money off your books?"

"I...uh...." Nora cleared her throat. "I make enough so that writing is my only job."

Another hand went up. "About how much money do you make off of each book?"

"It depends on what happens during the bidding process. I usually get a fairly healthy advance and my books earn out pretty quickly."

"What does that mean?" Asked the same Ugg girl.

"It means I have to sell enough copies of my book to make up for my advance before I start earning regular royalty checks."

Jacqueline stepped forward to rescue Nora from her apparent credit check. "Ok, how about we keep our questions focused on Ms. Phillips' writing and not on her paycheck?"

From the back of the room, Nora heard a muffled snicker and saw Selena hiding her face with her hand. Good to see someone was finding this amusing. She slowly raised her hand and waited for Nora to call on her.

"How do you plot out the actual murders in your books?" she asked.

Nora breathed a sigh of relief; finally a question she could answer in her sleep! "Generally I take bits and pieces from real crimes. Since I write cozy mysteries I don't have to go into the blood and guts part of it but I do have to make sure I see the investigation through so there are no loose ends. Otherwise, the reader feels cheated. Charlie fans expect a happy ending that includes the criminal being brought to justice and the whole thing neatly explained by the heroine."

There was a wave of giggling from the Ugg girls as one of them stage whispered, "Just like *Murder She Wrote*. What is she, Angela Lansbury?"

"Angela Lansbury was the main character on that show," Nora snapped. "She played a writer. She wasn't actually writing the episodes." She stopped just shy of calling the girls morons but Jacqueline jumped in anyway, just in case Nora found she couldn't hold her tongue.

"Alright, that's enough for today. Let's give Ms. Phillips a hand." Jacqueline turned to her and mouthed, *I'm sorry* as Nora gathered up the materials she had brought but never had a chance to share. Sporadic, half-hearted clapping erupted as the pod girls in their sweatpants grabbed their designer bags and tripped out the door in one giant glob. "I should have warned you about that group."

The last of the students were slowly packing up looking slightly unsure of what had just happened in class. "It's fine. It actually went better than I expected."

Jacqueline laughed. "Yeah. They have a one-track mind and clearly, it's not literature."

"Things have certainly changed since I was in your class, that's for sure. None of those kids even took notes."

"Except Selena of course." Jacqueline gestured towards the back of the room where Selena sat with her chin propped in her hand, watching the conversation between Nora and Jacqueline. She was making it obvious that she was waiting for Nora.

"Of course," Nora agreed. She wondered though if Selena was actually taking notes on Nora's lecture or if she was making notes on her own case. "I'm going to catch up with her actually. I have a feeling she's waiting for me."

Jacqueline raised an eyebrow. "Best of luck with that." She

disconnected her laptop from the projector and tucked it into her bag, then wound a chunky knit scarf around her neck. She threw Nora a tiny wave on her way out.

Selena rose from her desk and closed the distance between her and Nora. "That was a great presentation."

"Ha. You're kidding right?" *Had she been in the same room?* "That was awful."

"No, it wasn't awful. You just happened to be lecturing to a group that was 85% fake boobs."

Nora snorted. "Fair point. What can I do for you?"

"I was wondering if we could do some digging on those two news items?"

"Sure. Why not." Sighing, Nora muttered, "it's not like I have a novel to write or anything."

"What?"

"Nothing." Nora shook her head and hitched her bag up on her shoulder. "Let's start with school records. I'm still friendly with the president's secretary. They might have something on file that can give us some more information about one or the other of the girls."

They walked silently down the main staircase to the rotunda where they hung a left and headed for the president's office. President Keating's secretary Carol was tucked neatly behind her desk, her phone pressed to her ear. She spotted Nora in the doorway and wiggled her perfectly manicured fingers in her direction, gesturing for them to wait while she wrapped up her call.

Nora looked around and realized that Carol's office never changed. The faces in the group photos hanging on the wall might be different but everything else remained the same. She imagined Carol's office looked exactly as it did when the first president presided over the college. Even Carol herself never seemed to age, her perfect blond bob sprayed into shape and her lipstick the same shade of salmon it had been for every year Nora had known her. She was one of the kindest and most personable people Nora had ever met and she always had time to sit and chat whenever Nora dropped by.

"Nora!" She cried, hanging up the phone and pushing back from her desk. She came around with her arms spread wide to give Nora a hug— Carol was one of the few people who could get away with that level of physical contact- and pulled her close while rocking side to side on her tiptoes. Her head barely cleared Nora's shoulder but her personality was big enough to make up for her diminutive stature. "What brings you by?"

"Actually, I'm doing some research that you might be able to help with."

"Oh!" Carol breathed. "Is it for a new book?"

Nora locked eyes with Selena who nodded ever so slightly, granting Nora permission to stretch the truth. "Yes, for my new book. I'm thinking about setting it right here at Elms!"

"My oh my! That's fantastic! What can I do to help?"

"Well," Nora put her hand out, hoping Selena had the articles with her, smiling as Selena pulled them out of her bag. " Have you seen these before?" Nora showed Carol the two news items, then handed her the papers so she could look at them closer.

"I think I remember hearing something about this." Carol pushed her glasses up her nose and squinted at the paper, then shuffled to the other article. "Hang on just a second." She gave the papers back to Nora and went to a bank of filing cabinets, pulling open one of the drawers. She flipped through the tabbed folders until she found what she was looking for. "Here it is. The freshman girl who went missing on Elms Night was Celia Graves, a legacy. From what I understand her parents reported her missing but the case was closed a few days later. I assume she was eventually located but she never did return to campus." Carol turned and handed Nora a typewritten letter from Celia's family, apologizing for the trouble their daughter had caused.

Handing the letter off to Selena, Nora waited as Carol sifted through more folders. "And it looks like the girl who died on campus was Lillian Hanley, a senior at the time. According to notes from the campus nursing staff, she turned up at the infirmary one night complaining of feeling wretched, covered in bruises and red marks. Before anyone could ask her what happened, she was dead." She handed Nora a report from the infirmary. "It goes without saying that you didn't hear any of this from me. But you might want to ask some of the Sisters. There are a few who were here then as novices. They might remember something."

Selena finished taking notes on the letter from the Graves family and then traded it back to Nora for Lillian Hanley's infirmary record. "We heard nothing," she said with a wink as her pen flew across the pages of her notebook. Carol carefully tucked the note back into the filing cabinet from whence it came and waited while Selena finished with the infirmary notes.

"Do you think there's a story here?" Carol asked, watching Selena's intent scribbling.

"We're not sure yet. Selena here was doing some research on the history of the college and dug these up in the process."

Carol nodded. "Well I can't tell you whether or not there's anything more there but you've certainly caught my interest!"

Finished with the infirmary record, Selena reluctantly handed it back to Carol who quickly turned to the copy machine and shoved the document into the feeder, then waited as it whirred to life and spit out two slightly crooked copies. She pressed the pages into Selena's hands just as her phone rang. She waved us off with a wink as she picked up the call and sank into conversation. Selena tucked the record into her bag and secured the flap as if we might pass someone in the halls who would know what it was she had a copy of.

"Let's make a quick trip up to the fourth floor." Nora with a smile. "We can go pretend to check out the Catherine statue."

Laughing, Selena headed out of Carol's office and took a right. "You know that story isn't real."

"Of course not. But from the balcony, you can see the old library. It might give us some inspiration, imagining what things were like here when Lillian and Celia were students."

They crossed the Rotunda to the elevator where Nora pressed the call button like she had so many times when she was a student. The elevator dated back to the construction of Berchmans in 1932 with a metal cage that folded like an accordion, one that looked just like the elevator in Titanic, that opened to a trio of wooden panels that slid back to allow the rider onto the elevator. The thickness of the doors left such a gap that if you looked down you could see the entire elevator shaft below you. Nora often questioned the elevator's safety but as a lazy undergrad, safety hadn't exactly been her primary concern.

Instead, Nora had reveled in the romance of riding in an elevator that had its original Bakelite buttons and a panel that glowed with the light of ancient light bulbs, lighting each floor number as it climbed from the basement to the fourth floor. Oftentimes Nora and Margaret would come over to Berchmans in the late evening just to ride the elevator. During the day Nora only used it if she had ballet or art class in the basement where the small gym and studio spaces were. Her favorite was the art room in the very back corner where she had taken Word and Image with Professor Brunelle. In the winter that basement was the warmest part of the building because the boiler room around the corner from the studios fed the steam pipes that hid under loosely secured metal panels the whole length of the basement hallways to the radiators in the classrooms above.

But they weren't headed to the basement. Instead, Selena slid first the gate, then the wooden doors closed and pushed the button for the fourth floor where they found themselves overlooking what was once the college library but was now the Irish Cultural Center. Though the room below was what Nora wanted to see, they first took a small detour over to a relatively small white stone statue that was mounted to the rail overlooking the former library. It was a woman lying on her side and, as legend had it, that woman was Catherine, the oft-spoken of victim of foul play in Berchmans Hall. At some point in the statue's existence it had been broken, conveniently at the neck, and repaired so that the faintest hint of a fissure was still evident in the smooth white stone. As the story went, Catherine, for one reason or another, had leaped to her death from the bell tower that was hidden behind a locked door to the right of the statue. The story of why she jumped changed from generation to generation but the basic plot of the story remained the same: Catherine had sinned, a sin so great that she could not live with herself, and so she chose instead to end her life. Of course, the door to the bell tower had been locked ever since.

Nora reached out and touched the crack that wound itself around the woman's neck as she lay on her side as if napping in the sun. All of her stone edges were worn smooth— her fingers, the tip of her nose- from generations of Elms girls doing exactly what Nora was doing right now. Some touched the figure out of curiosity and perhaps dread, others rubbed the worn stone for luck before exams. There had even been a time or two when Nora had caught a faculty member doing the same and she wondered just how much of the legend they themselves believed, though they were quick to chase away any student caught lingering too long in that spot.

"So you never believed it?" Selena asked, breaking the silence.

Looking out over the cultural center, Nora shook her head, then laughed. "To be honest, we all believed it at first. And we repeated it gleefully to anyone who would listen. But the longer you're here, the more you settle in, the less likely you are to believe that kind of thing."

"I guess I can see that. I've only been here for a semester so everything about this campus is still new to me. It must be so easy for the upperclassmen to convince the first years that there's some great fog of mystery hanging over this place."

"I remember buying into that feeling." Nora smiled wistfully, thinking back to her first weeks on campus. Those few horrid months in the freshman dorm followed by the aggravation of packing up all her belongings yet again, to finding herself settled into one of the rooms that time forgot with her new roommate who became a lifelong friend. "I loved everything about this campus. And it just has that atmosphere to it I guess. That old wood, old academia feel."

"Did you major in English?"

"Education actually. I wanted to teach high school English and creative writing. And I did, for a while. Until my writing career finally became a reality."

"I'm majoring in history but I also want to be a writer."

"I sometimes wish I had majored in history myself," Nora replied, leaning forward to plant her elbows on the rail. A student was walking the hallway below her, probably headed for one of the science labs, and looked up as if she sensed Nora hanging above her. Did she worry Nora might suddenly fall? She smiled at the girl before turning back to Selena. "I love history. It's a big part of the reason I set the Charlie Donahue mysteries in a small town with a lot of it. Very New England. It just felt right for her to live somewhere where her fashion sense wasn't out of place, nor was her love of tradition and old-world values. Of course that was also thanks to my love of period British mysteries."

"That's my favorite thing about your books. Charlie is such a strong character but at the same time, she could have come right out of an episode of *Bewitched* with Samantha's perfect hair and gorgeous dresses. She strikes me as very mod."

"She would have been right at home on the set of that show," Nora laughed, imagining Charlie teaming up with Samantha to solve some mystery without Darren finding out. "If they ever made a series out of those books Charlie would have the quintessential mid-century modern cottage, complete with starburst wallpaper and a Formica-topped kitchen table."

Selena smiled broadly and leaned forward as well, mirroring Nora's posture. "I can see that. I know she's very rarely at home in the books but it's fun to imagine what her home life would be like."

"You know, you're right. She never is at home, is she? She's always at the bookshop or off on the trail of some suspect or other." She turned and looked at Selena in disbelief. "Maybe that's what my next book should be. Charlie at home!" She laughed so loud that someone from down below shushed her which only made her laugh harder. Soon she and Selena were both giggling helplessly. "We came up here to see the library and here we are practically writing the next Charlie Donahue novel. Charlie would have loved the original library." She shook her head and glanced down at her watch. "I should really get going."

"Me too," Selena agreed, pushing away from the rail.

They climbed back into the elevator and rode it to the first floor where Nora reached into her bag for one of her business cards. "Here," she said, scribbling a number on the back. "This is my cell number. If you can't find me here on campus, feel free to call me. Maybe later this week we can head over to the newspaper archives and give it a second look."

"That would be great." Selena took the card and slipped it into her pocket. "I'm headed this way." She gestured towards the quad while Nora was parked in the lot behind Admissions in the opposite direction.

Chapter Six

Though Nora would have preferred to head home right then, she knew she should take the time to get in the pool. Her aching knee was a reminder that she had been lazy this week and hadn't moved nearly enough. She unlocked her car and dragged her bag from the back seat, then followed the sidewalk in front of the chapel and around to the Maguire Center.

When she was first applying to undergrad as a high school senior she hadn't known exactly what it was she was looking for in a college. She knew she wanted a picturesque campus but after touring a number of other schools, she also realized she wanted something small, something rather intimate. She had zero interest in a place like the University of Massachusetts. Any campus that resembled a small city in itself was too overwhelming and didn't fit Nora's vision of the quaint New England campus she had conjured in her fantasies.

She had done an overnight visit at both Assumption and Mount Holyoke but neither one felt right to her. It wasn't until she did an overnight at Elms that she felt she had found someplace she could call home. The campus had less than 300 students and only four buildings, not counting the chapel. With only two dorms, very few students lived there and there was still the option of having a single room as an upperclassman. Class sizes were small, the professors knew their students by name, and everything about Elms screamed tradition.

Nora would never forget her first Elms Night celebration. Though it was the first year they had broken tradition with a coed freshman class, the magic of Elms Night seemed to erase all of No-

61

ra's doubts about having chosen the Elms. She stood in the middle of the rotunda with the rest of the first years and stared up into the faces of the senior girls lined up along the rail above, swaying and singing their class song. The lights in the rotunda sparkled like starshine as the seniors reached out and let pristine beanies fall from their fingers and flutter down and down into the outstretched hands of the first years below.

Her beanie was now tucked away with her lanyard and her tassel along with a beautiful drawing of O'Leary Hall somewhere that she had just never gotten around to framing but that she treasured nonetheless. She wondered then if they still carried on with the same traditions like assigning each first year a big sister— though she supposed there would now be plenty of big brothers too. Did they still do Soph Show? she wondered. That had been one of her favorite events, when the sophomore class put on a show for their senior big sisters as a graduation gift. Every show had a theme and theirs had been The Wizard of Elmstock. Nora had long since forgotten the reasoning behind it but she was pretty sure she still had the t-shirt packed away somewhere.

When she got to the pool she found it empty, just the way she liked it, and she eased herself into the water. Her walk down memory lane hadn't been nearly enough exercise for her poor knee and she knew she was going to have to ice it for quite a while when she got home or else it would keep her up all night. She tried to take it slow as she glided through the water from one end of the pool to the other and back again.

The sound of the locker room door slamming shut nearly made her jump out of her skin as she grabbed for the edge of the deck on the opposite end of the pool. Nora looked up to see Sister Eleanor dropping her towel on the bleachers before heading for the shallow end of the pool nearest Nora and carefully wading in.

"Nora! Fancy meeting you here."

"Hello Sister. Come here often?"

The nun smirked at Nora's feeble joke. "Not as often as I should but then my dance card isn't nearly as full as yours."

"I don't get here often enough either, as my knee will likely attest." Nora kicked her legs slowly as she hung from the rounded edge of the pool. Her knee was already protesting the exercise but she knew if she didn't keep it moving it would get stiff enough to make it difficult to get out of the water.

Sister Eleanor took a few more steps into the water until it was at her waist, then bent her knees until her chin touched the water. "So Carol tells me you stopped in to see her today."

"News travels fast around here, doesn't it?"

"Carol and I eat lunch together most days. She said you brought along a girl she didn't recognize? A first year?"

Nora nodded. "Selena. I don't know her last name but I met her in Jacqueline's class. She's a fan."

"Mmm. I hear she's also a fan of our local folklore."

"I wouldn't necessarily say folklore. More accurately she's a budding writer searching for her story and she thinks this campus is it." Nora turned around and spread her arms across the deck so she could stretch her legs out in front of her. Her kneecaps bobbed to the surface, her toes poking out of the water. "It's become a bit of an obsession."

"And you're encouraging her to dig into whatever it is she thinks she's found?" Sister Eleanor was looking at her strangely, as if Nora had just told her she was encouraging Selena to explore Satanism.

"And what if I am?"

"Then you're a fool."

Nora barked out a laugh then quickly covered her mouth, but it was too late. She had laughed at a nun. And not just any nun, the most formidable nun she had ever met. By the time Nora was a student at the Elms the nuns were few and far between. The school itself was slowly moving towards becoming more secular, separating itself from its decidedly Catholic roots. Even the name had been shortened from the College of Our Lady of the Elms to simply Elms College. Sister Eleanor taught World Religions which, when Nora arrived as a first year, was still a required course.

"I'm sorry. I don't mean to laugh but that's not at all what I expected you to say!"

"Did you expect me to say I take no issue with you helping a student 'investigate' this campus? That you're lending credence to this girl's suggestion not only that someone was killed but that the church somehow covered it up?" Sister Eleanor's mouth flattened into a frown, a look of disappointment that Nora had never seen pointed in her direction before. "I most certainly do take issue."

"I'm sorry you feel that way Sister but don't you think if there's something there, if someone really was hurt or perhaps even murdered, we owe it to them to find out what happened?"

"I was here, you know. When Celia Graves went missing. And when Lillian Hanley died. Both those girls' families worked hard to put all that behind them. It's absurd to drag it all up again and cast suspicion on two unconnected incidents, both of which were settled long ago."

"And you've never had any doubt about either girl?" Nora had peeled herself off of the side of the pool and slowly made her way into the shallow end, nearer to Sister Eleanor. Partly because she wanted to sit on the steps and give her knee a rest, and partly because she wanted to close the physical distance between them as Eleanor's tone grew harsher. "I heard Celia Graves never returned. And that Lillian Hanley had bruises that were never explained."

Sister Eleanor shook her head vehemently. "Absolutely not.

Miss Graves didn't return due to sheer embarrassment. She left campus with a boy which was against the rules back then, and she did it very publicly." A bead of sweat ran down the bridge of Sister Eleanor's nose and she reached up to wipe it away, swiping it to the side which made her look like she had been crying. "And Lillian Hanley's death was unfortunate but certainly not foul play."

"But no one was able to produce an explanation for the bruises. Or the sudden onset of her illness for that matter."

Sister Eleanor finally came over and joined her on the steps. "Nora, I have a great deal of respect for you and for the work you do. It's only right that you should want to take a young writer under your wing but there's no story here."

Nora stared straight ahead, watching the water ripple against the wall at the opposite end of the pool.

"You need to encourage this girl to leave this story alone. For everyone's sake."

"And what happens if I don't?"

"Well, at the very least all the relationships you value here on campus will dissolve. No one will accept you digging into the school's history like this."

Rather than continue to poke at it, Nora chose a different tack and changed the subject. "You knew both girls?"

Nora looked over to see that Sister Eleanor's expression had changed, her face clouded over. Sister Eleanor nodded slowly. "I did. I was still rather new here when Lillian started as a first year. I was low man on the totem pole, just a teaching assistant in those early years, but the minute I met Lillian I knew she was something special."

"What was she like?"

"She was very smart, smarter than most of the girls in her class. She had graduated from high school a year early so she was younger but she was somehow more mature than the others. It wasn't surprising that she was named head girl her senior year. That would have been 1953. By the spring of that next year she was gone."

Nora wasn't sure just how much she could ask of Sister Eleanor. The topic of Lillian's death was understandably upsetting but Nora's curiosity threatened to get the better of her. "How well did you get to know her?"

"I ran a tutoring program where we matched the brighter girls with those who were struggling in some of their academics. Lillian excelled in just about everything and she was by far my best tutor."

"Carol told me no one realized Lillian was sick?"

Sister Eleanor nodded again. "It was late May if I remember correctly." She sighed and scratched at an invisible itch on the front of her knee. "No one had any idea that Lillian had been sick. She hadn't missed any classes and she was keeping up with her responsibilities as head girl— planning social activities and the like. Then one night she showed up in the infirmary, white as a sheet and barely able to stand. I don't even know how she made it there."

"I find it hard to believe," Nora interrupted, "that she got that sick that fast without anyone noticing."

"We all wondered the same thing, believe me. How could none of us have noticed something was wrong?" She crossed her arms over her chest and shivered. "Especially me. I spent the most time with her out of everyone on the faculty, supervising her tutoring duties and reviewing her assignments for the classes I assisted in. I always thought there should have been some sign."

"It sounds to me like Lillian wasn't one to complain." Lillian sounded like a Type A perfectionist who would be loath to admit that something was wrong. Especially if that something took her away from her responsibilities. "Maybe she just hid it well."

Eleanor shook her head. "No, that wasn't possible. When she died, we were told that her organs were so damaged that there was no way she could have passed for healthy. She would have been severely jaundiced and wouldn't have had the energy to make it down the stairs in O'Leary, nevermind attend to her regular activities. Yet no one was ever able to present an alternate theory that suited her symptoms. What fast-acting illness came on, intensified, and killed in the space of twelve hours?"

"How do you know it was twelve hours from onset?"

"I had seen Lillian earlier that morning. Very early in fact." Eleanor reached up again to scratch her nose. "It must have been about 5:00 in the morning. She was out walking the fields where the Maguire Center is now, getting in a bit of exercise, she said. I was on my way back to the residence at the back of campus after having unlocked the chapel."

So she had seen Lillian, healthy as could be, moving on her own steam, mere hours before she showed up in the infirmary with some mysterious illness. "She was just fine then. And by evening she was on death's door. Quite literally."

Eleanor had no idea what could have killed Lillian and as far as she knew no autopsy was performed as there was no suspicion of foul play. As far as the college was concerned, Lillian had contracted some sort of fast-acting illness and thus died of natural causes.

"It sounds to me like you actually do have doubts." Nora said pointedly. "Just like Selena."

Sister Eleanor didn't answer right away. Instead she went for that spot on her knee again, then recrossed her arms. She was definitely feeling defensive about something but Nora had no idea what. "I wouldn't necessarily say doubts. Not like your little protegé, not as if there was foul play involved. I simply have a hard time believing that Lillian died from some sort of illness that didn't seem to infect anyone else. Not even her roommates. I would think that any sickness that virulent would also be highly contagious."

"You make a good point. Did anyone follow up on this illness?"

She shook her head sadly. "No they didn't. It was case closed as far as they were concerned."

"And what about Celia? Did no one find it odd that now two girls were mysteriously taken from the Elms campus?"

Sister Eleanor looked confused. "What would one have to do with the other? And Celia wasn't missing. She just didn't come back to campus."

"There was a piece in the paper about Elms Night, dated 1953— Lillian's senior year. On the night of the celebration a first year student fled the event and got in a stranger's car never to be seen again. Are you sure it was her choice not to return?" Nora wondered if perhaps the nuns had been fed a tall tale about Celia. "Supposedly Lillian heard the girl scream that night."

"She never mentioned it to me. And we were told the girl was located. There was never any search, no further discussion of it amongst the staff or administration that I know of."

"Were you told directly, explicitly that she had been found? Suppose the girl wasn't found. That makes for a very strange set of coincidences does it not? Especially if Lillian truly did hear a scream coming from that car."

Nora was surprised that Sister Eleanor was still entertaining her questions given her initial reaction to Nora's digging. She wasn't surprised Carol had told her about Nora and Selena's visit– it was a small, tight-knit campus and someone digging into these two girls' lives would without doubt raise a few eyebrows- but she was surprised that Eleanor felt so strongly about it.

"Sister, I honestly think Selena might be on to something here and if there's any chance that the circumstances between Celia Graves and Lillian Hanley are connected…" Nora pulled herself out of the pool and headed for her towel that was neatly folded next to where Sister Eleanor had dropped hers.

"Then you think you're the one who should make that connection? You're going to look into this no matter what I say aren't you?"

"Well I'm certainly not leaving it up to a first year to unravel on her own."

Sister Eleanor gave her a sad smile. "Then on your head be it. Don't say I didn't warn you."

Nora threw the nun a mock salute and headed for the locker room. Damn straight she was going to look into this. Sister Eleanor's warning just made her want it more and she could feel herself developing the same tunnel vision she had wanted Selena about but the groundwork was there and it was time for a professional to step in to put the pieces together. And Nora knew just the professional.

CHAPTER SEVEN

Over the course of her writing career Nora had made a good many useful connections. Most of those connections were in academia: professors, librarians, museum curators. But then there were her law enforcement connections. When she started writing the first Charlie Donahue mystery she reached out to a high school friend who was now a detective to make sure she was getting the procedural details right. Lucky for her he never seemed to get tired of her calling and asking questions about stalking laws or how to track a suspect who disappears from a car wreck. But this time she wasn't going to him with a hypothetical. She called the station and asked for Detective Dave Morris.

"What crazy story have you concocted this time?" Dave always teased her like this when she called but only minutes into her explanation, he grew quiet. He could tell this was serious. "Let me ask you something. Is this for a new novel? Or is this something else entirely?"

She paused, unsure how to answer. "I don't know. I think it's both. But it's certainly not the usual run of the mill stuff I use in my books. I'd rather just run it by you in person."

"I'm off at 7:00. How about we discuss this over a beer?"

"Sounds good." They settled on a bar in their old neighborhood, one Nora could never remember the name of but everyone knew exactly where it was. In fact it was less than a block away from her parents' house, the house she had grown up in. Most of her friends had stayed in town after graduation or returned shortly after finishing college. Their town was one of those you spent your entire adolescence longing to escape, then your entire adulthood working to get back to.

The place was crowded for a weekday but Nora chalked it up to the cold. Nearly everyone in there was cradling a mug of something hot and alcoholic while they chatted and watched whatever inane game show was on the big screen over the bar. Dave had already claimed a stool and ordered a beer when Nora slid in next to him, trying to get the bartender's attention.

"It's about time you showed up," Dave said, tipping his half-empty beer in her direction.

Nora looked down at her watch and frowned. "It's 6:55. You said you got off at 7:00 so technically I'm still early."

"Yeah yeah. So what have you got for me?"

The bartender wandered over and took Nora's order for an Irish coffee. Seeing everyone else with their mugs full of foamy, boozy goodness made her want one too so she broke down and asked for hers with a shot of Jameson and a shot of Baileys. "And sugar too please."

"Are you *trying* to give yourself diabetes?"

"And cirrhosis. I figured I would get it all at once, just take care of it in one fell swoop." Nora reached into her bag and pulled out her notes along with copies of the original news pieces Selena had found in the basement. "Ok. So I don't know how much information you can give me and it might be nothing more than a long shot. But I came across these two articles, just margin notes really, but they caught my eye. Then I did some digging in student records." Dave raised an eyebrow. "Don't ask."

She handed the papers over to Dave and sipped her coffee while he read both pieces. Nora had written the girls' names above each piece and then stapled the copies, along with the copies of the infirmary record, to her own notes. She watched Dave flip each page and carefully skim the next. When he was finished, he turned the pages back to the beginning and placed them flat on the bar, his hands folded on top of them while he thought.

"Well? What do you think?"

Dave sighed and picked up the papers again, flipping quickly through for a second time. "I think you have a girl who took off with a boyfriend in 1953. And another girl who died from an unfortunate illness early the next year. What makes you think they're linked?"

"Did you see my note about the dead girl having heard the missing girl scream the night she left campus?"

"Yes I did. And I think it's flimsy at best."

"I know it is but something is nagging at me." Nora signaled the bartender and asked him for a water to wash down her *more Irish than usual* Irish coffee. "Can you just look into it for me?"

"Sure," he waved the papers. "These are copies right?"

Nora nodded. She had her original notes and copies tucked safely in her bag. "Thanks. I appreciate it."

"Not a problem." Dave rolled the papers up and tucked them in the inside pocket of his coat just as a group of his fellow officers came spilling through the front door of the bar.

"And that's my cue! Have a good night." Nora peeled a few ones out of her wallet and dropped them on the bar, then headed home where she found a quiche waiting for her on her porch, a note from her mother taped to the cover with directions for reheating. She loved her mother's cooking and there was no way she was going to pass up the famous Phillips quiche. Nora cranked up the heat and turned on the TV for noise while she busied herself in the kitchen reheating a slice of heaven. These were the days when she loved living mere blocks away from her parents.

Nora didn't realize how tired she was until she sank into the couch and Luna hopped up, took a few turns, then curled into a ball next to her. With the warmth of the dog snuggled up next to her coupled with the droning buzz of the TV, Nora felt her eyelids start to droop and she drifted off to sleep. She rarely fell asleep on the couch but on the rare occasions that she did, it was hardly a comfortable sleep, or a deep sleep. Instead, she was subconsciously aware that she was sleeping in a rather uncomfortable position that would likely result in both a crick in her neck and pain in her knee when she inevitably woke up in the middle of the night wanting her bed.

As she slept fitfully, readjusting her aching knee, trying to shift Luna enough to get comfortable, she floated in a dream world where she was walking the Elms campus as a student, not in the 90s like she actually had, but in the 50s. She was standing in the rotunda, looking up at a face she had never seen before but she somehow knew instinctually was Lillian Hanley's. Behind her the doors to Berchmans Hall slammed shut and she heard a scream from outside that was so loud it echoed off the stone staircases and bounced around the cathedral ceiling that rose high above Lillian's head. Nora turned and pushed the doors open again, running out to the front gate where she could see the taillights of an unidentified car disappearing into the night.

CHAPTER EIGHT

The next morning Nora made herself a cup of tea and headed upstairs to her office. It wasn't exactly a room per se, more like a storage loft that was just big enough for a desk, a chair, and a few low bookcases. She had laid out a fluffy shag rug and thrown a couple of floor pillows down against the wall, wedged under the one and only window in the room. It was tiny but cozy, the perfect place for plotting out her next novel. *If only she had an idea she could run with.*

It had only been a week since Eric's phone call but it somehow felt like it had been months, years even since he had laid down his ultimatum: *another Charlie Donahue book or else*. Or else this cute little office would soon be boxed up and stored away because she wouldn't have enough money to cover her mortgage and would have to move back in with her parents. Nora looked around at her books, all neatly shelved, looking absolutely pristine, and imagined them stuffed in a cardboard box where they wouldn't see the light of day maybe for months.

Normally, when she was plotting out a new book she would jot down notes about settings, characters, plot and then stick those notes on the wall above her desk along with newspaper clippings that inspired some of the crimes Charlie Donahue investigated, quotes from books and articles, sometimes photos of gravestones with interesting names Nora thought she might use for secondary characters. By the time she was well into the manuscript, the entire wall would be covered and she would spend days shuffling things around, sometimes discarding the pieces that no longer fit as the plot evolved. It was the only part of her process that resembled planning. The rest was just flying by the seat of her pants, writing what came to her and worrying about continuity later.

This time her wall was bare, the last set of notes from the last book tucked neatly away in a file box that held the research from every manuscript she'd written over the course of her career. Now she grabbed a new pile of multicolored Post-It notes and started recording what little she and Selena had learned so far about Lillian Hanley and her connection to the missing girl. Dave was right– it was flimsy; so flimsy that Nora worried the whole idea might snap at any minute, but her instinct told her there was something, had to be something. With any luck, Dave would come up with enough information for Nora to connect the dots.

After sticking the notes to the wall, Nora sat back and stared at them until the edges of the paper began to blur and her head began to ache. Then, suddenly, Nora felt something click into place and she grabbed her laptop, opened up a fresh document, and started typing, typing everything she could think of about Elms, about the Catherine legend, about Celia and Lillian, the times they lived in and what life at Elms was like in 1953. Nora imagined what that Elms Night celebration would have looked like, sounded like, felt like for Lillian Hanley who had probably been dreaming of becoming head girl since the day she set foot on campus. Then she wondered what that same night had been like for Celia Graves. Had she really left willingly with a boyfriend? Or had that scream meant something sinister?

Nora recalled everything Sister Eleanor had told her about Lillian and built her out like she would any other character in any other Charlie Donahue novel as she realized she was writing not from her own perspective, but from Charlie's. Then she dropped Charlie into the center of the campus, into the heart of the mystery, where she met a student that bore an uncanny resemblance to Selena. For the first time ever Charlie Donahue had a sidekick. Nora's main character suddenly became part of a duo.

Nearly two hours later Nora rose from her chair and stretched. Hank had wandered up to join her in her office and had fallen asleep on one of the floor pillows. He looked up at her and yawned, mimicking her stretch. Nora slid down onto the other pillow and stroked his silky black fur until he reached over his shoulder and bared his teeth at her, which meant one more stroke and he would latch onto her knuckles, their love fest over with. Hank had drawn blood enough times for Nora to know she didn't want to push him. Instead, she leaned against the wall and closed her eyes, suddenly very tired.

She must have dozed off, waking to the sound of her cell phone buzzing away on her desk. Without thinking Nora rolled over and tried to get to her knees, forgetting for a moment that she was still recovering from surgery. She winced and fell over on her side as the phone continued to buzz, though if she waited much longer she would miss the call. Scooting on her side until she was close enough to the desk to use it to pull herself up, Nora let out a mighty groan as she used the edge of the desk to get to her feet just in time to see Dave's number flash across the screen.

"Rats." She had missed the call. Snatching the phone, she waited for the voicemail notification.

"Nora, it's Dave. I found something rather interesting about your two girls. Give me a call when you can."

Dialing Dave's number, Nora shook with impatience as she listened to it ring over and over again until she got his voicemail. "Of course," she muttered, waiting for the tone to leave her message. "Hi Dave, sorry I missed you. I couldn't get to the phone in time. Give me a call back when you can."

She hung up and slammed her cell phone down so hard that Hank jumped up and ran down the stairs. A moment later the phone rang again and Nora snatched it up, hoping it would be Dave but she didn't recognize the number this time.

"Hello?"

"Ms. Phillips?"

"Yes, this is. Who may I ask is calling?"

The person on the other end of the line paused. "This is Betty Farraday. I went to school with Lillian Hanley. Elms College, class of 1954."

Nora's heart stopped for a moment, then slammed back to life, hammering against her chest. "Ms. Farraday. How did you get my number?"

"Oh Carol called me. Said you were asking questions about Lillian for your next book?" Betty chuckled, cleared her throat. "I've read all your books and if I can be of any help, I'd be just delighted."

"Thank you," Nora replied, breathless. "That would be wonderful."

"I don't get out much anymore," she explained, "but you'd be more than welcome to come over here for tea."

"That would be lovely. Where can I find you?"

Betty gave an address that was only a few blocks away from the college in one of the quiet little neighborhoods tucked in on the other side of Springfield Street. When Nora got to her house, she found a cozy little cottage with the obligatory white picket fence, neatly tended flower gardens that were wintering over nicely, and perfectly trimmed shrubs. Betty was waiting at the door when Nora pulled into her driveway, holding open the storm as Nora grabbed her bag and locked her car.

"Come on in! I've got the kettle on to boil and made some fresh sugar cookies." Betty's house looked and smelled like perpetual Christmas. The holiday had long since gone by but judging by the coating of dust on nearly every reindeer and Santa's elf on Betty's mantle, those decorations were out year round. A candle that smelled of fir trees was burning on the coffee table and a plate of sugar cookies was laid out on a tree-shaped platter with a paper lace doily. Betty bustled around the kitchen getting down mugs decorated with snowflakes and a red sugar bowl that looked like it was straight out of the 1950s. Actually, now that she was looking around, she realized that everything in Betty's house was from the 50s.

"These cookies smell amazing," Nora called as the kettle began to whistle. She poked her head in the kitchen and asked if Betty needed any help but the woman shook her head.

"I may be old but I'm not dead yet. I can still put on the dog when I need to." Betty turned and handed Nora a steaming cup of hot tea. "It's not every day I have a famous author coming to visit me."

Nora followed Betty into the living room where she lowered herself onto the pink upholstered couch and gestured for Nora to take one of the gold wingback chairs that were positioned on the other side of the coffee table.

"Thank you so much for calling me and having me over. I'm very much looking forward to hearing what you know about Lillian."

Betty leaned back on the couch and took a sip of her tea. "Lillian and I were roommates our freshman year. By the time the year was over, we were best friends." She gazed off into the middle distance as she remembered those early days at Elms. "Back then it wasn't common for girls to go to college. You had to have money and standing in order to send your daughter to a place like Elms. We had dorm mothers and curfews, and we were never out of sight of the nuns but we didn't mind. We were just happy to have a small taste of what we thought of as the real world."

Taking another sip of tea, Betty reached for a pile of books that were perched on the side table next to the couch. She paged through one of them and handed it to Nora. "That's Lillian," she said, tapping on the girl's class picture. "And that's me on the page before."

Seeing Lillian's face for the first time reminded Nora that, though she had gotten swept up in writing this story in from the comfort of her own home, Lillian had been a real person. A real girl who had gone away to college full of hopes and dreams only to wind up dead before graduation.

"What was she like?"

"Oh," Betty sighed. "She was unlike anyone else I had ever met. Headstrong, brilliant, and so kind. I was scared witless when I got to the Elms. I had never been away from home and even though my parents lived only a few miles away in Atwater Park, just down the street, I was terrified of being on my own. Lillian wasn't scared though. She took me under her wing and showed me how to be independent, how to be a grown up. She had class, boy did she have class." Betty shook her head and smiled sadly. "She was one of a kind, that girl."

"Betty, I'm sure it's hard for you to talk about, but can you tell me what happened the night she died?"

At first Betty didn't say anything and Nora wondered if she was going to clam up, if these memories were too difficult for her to talk about, but it seemed she was only gathering her thoughts. "To this day I still don't understand what happened to her. One minute she was just fine, laughing and happy. Then she was gone."

"How long was it actually? Between the time she was just fine and the time she went to the infirmary?"

"It was only the space of an afternoon if I remember correctly." Shifting in her seat, Betty nervously reached up to smooth her thinning white hair but was unable to tame the little wisps that had escaped the combs keeping her hair out of her face. "I didn't see her the evening she went to the infirmary. The last time I saw her was at breakfast that morning. We had both gotten pancakes in the refectory, then headed off to our morning classes. She was majoring in history and I was majoring in English. Since we were seniors we didn't have any classes together anymore so most days we only met up for meals."

"But you didn't see her at lunch?"

Betty shook her head. "On Fridays our schedules didn't match up so breakfast was the only time I would have seen her."

"And she was fine?"

"Completely fine. She ate everything on her plate while we chatted about plans for the weekend. Neither of us was planning to go home that weekend so we were trying to decide between a Saturday night movie or shopping."

From what Betty had heard, Lillian had started feeling poorly that afternoon. Other girls who were in class with her said it seemed to come on quickly. She sat in class looking green around the edges, then suddenly all color had drained from her face, but she didn't want to go to the infirmary. She just put it down to stress. She was going to be valedictorian and it was a lot of work keeping up her grades along with her social commitments. Lillian belonged to every important club on campus and was editor of the yearbook *and* the school paper. It was a miracle she had time to sleep.

By evening Lillian could barely pull herself out of her desk in her last class. Everyone else had headed off to the dorm to settle in for the night while Lillian was sitting alone in the classroom, her head on her outstretched arm. The custodian found her when he came to empty the trash and had picked her up, slinging her over his shoulder, and carried her to the infirmary but it was too late.

"By the time she got there, there was nothing left for them to do. Whatever had taken her had been slow, painful, and thorough."

"This might be a difficult question but was there an autopsy?"

"I don't know actually. It wasn't considered a suspicious death so they might not have thought to look into it."

"Did they ever determine a cause?"

"No, they just said she had contracted some sort of virus."

"Did you know Celia Graves?"

Betty looked surprised by the question but she answered immediately. "Oh yes. I saw everything that happened with that girl on Elms Night." She reached up and patted her hair again, clearly a nervous habit. "I had the perfect vantage point for the whole thing."

Betty remembered seeing Celia Graves walk into the rotunda with the other first years and, at the time, she hadn't taken much notice of her in particular; she was just enjoying watching a new class of Elms girls coming together in one place. But then she saw one of the nuns grab Celia roughly by the arm and pull her close, whispering something in her ear. "Of course the nuns were in their full habits and whoever it was had her back to me. I don't know who it was that talked to her but right after that, Celia ran out the front doors and that was the last we saw of her. Lillian didn't notice anything was wrong until Celia was already out the door. She said she saw the girl from the corner of her eye." That was when Lillian had left the building through the side door and had seen Celia get in that car, the one that ripped around the corner and jumped the curb out front. "Lillian closed the doors but by then I had run down after her. She didn't notice that I had followed but I had, and I heard that girl scream just like she did. Clear as day."

"Was there any follow up after she went missing?" Nora asked. "Did anyone say where she went or if she was found safe?"

Betty thought for a moment, her hands going to her hair yet again. "Come to think of it, the only thing we heard was from Sister Eleanor. She said the girl had been found but we never heard where or how. In fact, now that you mention it, I don't even know if she was found alive."

That was exactly what Nora was just thinking. Saying the girl had been "found" could have meant any number of things. She could have been safe and sound, dropped off in front of her parents' house. Or she could have been found down by the river, dead as can be. It was quite a vague statement indeed.

"Thank you so much for your time Betty. This has helped immensely."

"Oh, well." She seemed to momentarily forget what they were talking about, what it was Nora was thanking her for, but she recovered herself and smiled warmly. "I'm so glad dear. Now when do you think this book will be out?"

For a moment Nora forgot that had been the lie that got her in the front door in the first place. "Sometime next year I would think."

"That's so nice dear. I can't wait to read it!"

Just as Nora climbed into her car her phone rang. "Hey. Sorry I missed you before. I stupidly sat down on the floor and couldn't get up."

On the other end of the line Dave laughed while tapping away on his keyboard. He had to be calling from the station on a break. "We're going to have to get you a Life Call button like all the other old ladies."

"Go ahead. I'll make sure it links directly to you so you have to deal with me every time I'm stuck on the floor."

"Ha, good luck with that." Nora knew Dave would have no issue leaving her on the floor to starve to death and have her eyeballs eaten by Hank. "So I got some information on those two girls. It wasn't easy and I had to jump through a few hoops."

Nora put the car in gear and navigated out onto Springfield Street, heading for home. "What do you mean hoops?"

"It turns out your girl Lillian Hanley was pretty well connected. Her father was a big time local politician. Mother was a society maven."

"So they had a lot of pull in other words."

"You could say that. In fact they had enough pull to have whatever investigation there was into her death buried." Nora could hear Dave shuffling papers, pecking something out on his computer, then taking a sip of something. "It turns out the nurse in the infirmary had some doubts about how the girl died so she called the police before calling the parents. The cops show up, they start to ask questions, but they get shut down as soon as the parents show up. The body gets taken to Springfield Hospital. The story of a mystery virus spreads like wildfire."

"Which means there wasn't an autopsy."

Dave cleared his throat. "Actually, that's where things get a little weird. There was an autopsy. The hospital quietly called the medical examiner but the findings were never made public, never added to her file."

It was hard to believe that something like autopsy results would be hidden like that. "Did the autopsy support the virus theory?"

"No. Not at all."

"Then what did it conclude?"

"Get ready for this. She was poisoned."

1953

Betty Farraday was a terrible student. The only reason she was about to graduate with her class was because of Lillian Hanley. They had gone to high school together at Cathedral and Lillian had recognized almost immediately that Betty was struggling in school, that she couldn't read as well as the others, couldn't reason out a math problem as quickly, and her writing was atrocious. Lillian took Betty under her wing, helping her get through high school, then the college application process.

"You should come to the Elms with me," Lillian had said as went through one of Betty's homework assignments, erasing incorrect answers so she could go through them again with her. "I think you'd like it there. We're already used to uniforms and nuns so why not? Plus it's all girls so you wouldn't have to worry about keeping up with boys in the classes."

Betty nodded, only half listening as she watched Lillian decimate her math homework. "What you're really saying," she said as Lillian handed the sheet back to her, "is that the only way I'm going to survive college is if I have you to help me."

Lillian gave her a look but realized quickly that Betty's statement wasn't made out of self pity. She was simply stating a fact.

"And you'd be right," Betty continued, looking at her paper that was now mostly blank thanks to Lillian's eraser. "I need all the help I can get, clearly."

Lillian was Betty's saving grace and she knew it. They were polar opposites, Betty and Lillian. The Hanleys had made sure that Lillian always did her homework, paid for tutors when she needed a little extra help, enrolled her in extra curriculars. Betty's parents had no idea what to do with their daughter who didn't seem to be able to understand anything. Her mother would sigh and say, "At least you're pretty. You'll still get a husband. Men don't mind stupid women."

Betty didn't think her mother meant to hurt her feelings; she was just being practical like most women of her generation. It didn't matter if you finished school as long as you graduated with your Mrs. but being around Lillian made Betty wonder what it would be like to have something waiting for you other than marriage and children.

That was what Betty admired most about Lillian: she had a plan, a plan that was all her own and she had no intention of cutting it short just because she met an eligible man. She would grow up knowing she didn't need to rely on anyone but herself, something Betty knew she would never experience. Betty would always need someone to rely on— first her parents, then Lillian. Sometimes she wondered what the point was of going on to college but here she was, in her final year at the Elms.

She stood next to Lillian, leaning over the balcony and watching the first years crowd into the rotunda for the very last time. It was the last Elms Night they would ever have and they were finally on top, the ones who would welcome in the new class by dropping beanies from the second floor. They finally got to be the bearers of tradition, the girls who opened the new school year because in a few short months, they would also be the ones to close out the school year.

Elms Night was magical. The lights, the same lights that illuminated Berchmans every day, seemed to shine so much brighter that night. Betty might have even said they twinkled a bit, especially when they were reflected back to her in the eyes of so many first years, staring up in wonder at the senior girls above. Betty was about to say something about the lights when, out of the corner of her eye, she caught a bit of commotion near the door where the last of the first years were stumbling into the rotunda. She looked to her left and realized Lillian had seen it too— the nun grabbing one of the girls by the elbow and pulling her aside. She and Lillian both watched for the briefest moment as the girl's eyes went wide and, shaking off the nun's grip, darted out the front door. Before Betty could react, Lillian was already pushing through the other seniors and heading for the back stairs.

Betty took off after her but Lillian was too fast. She was already out the door and rounding the corner of the building by the time Betty made it down to the first floor. Stopping briefly on the stairs outside as the doors closed behind her, Betty looked up and out across the quad to Gaylord Street where she caught a glimpse of a green blazer heading towards a black car with a young man in the driver's seat. Shaking her head, Betty muttered, "Good riddance to bad trash then," as she assumed the girl would take off with this boy, behavior that was not at all permitted at Elms, but as she tripped down the stairs, intent on catching up with Lillian, something made her stop and look again.

The girl, whose profile she could now see, was not headed towards the passenger side of the car as she would be if she was expecting a ride. Instead she was headed for the driver who had rolled down the window in order to hear the girl whose arms waved in the dark as a brief breeze caught the edge of her skirt and pulled it behind her as if trying to pull her away from the car. The breeze also carried the girl's voice back to Betty and though she couldn't make out the words she could certainly make out the tone and the girl was not at all happy.

Suddenly the driver's side door wrenched open with a nasty squeal, the sound of metal grinding on metal with nothing to quiet it, and the driver lurched out onto the pavement until he was standing nose to nose with the girl. Betty watched as he grabbed her shoulders and shook her once, twice, a third time like a ragdoll, then spun her around and shoved her into the car. It looked as if the girl had lost her balance, giving the driver the advantage of being able to bundle her into the car, pushing and shoving her limbs until she fit.

Betty watched as the driver slid in after, slamming the door shut and abruptly putting the car in gear. She expected the girl to sit up at some point, right herself in the passenger seat, but she never did and the car took off like a shot, careening around the corner towards the front of Berchmans. Betty took off at a run and got to the front of the building just as the car barreled around the corner. Lillian had managed to close the front doors of Berchmans just as the girl in the car screamed.

Gasping for breath, Betty met Lillian as she headed for the side door to return to the festivities inside. "What on earth was that?" she said, bending over to rest her hands on her knees.

"Search me," Lillian shrugged, pushing her hands into the pockets of her blazer. "If I had to hazard a guess, that first year just left with a gentleman caller of less than desirable standing." She wiggled her eyebrows salaciously, making Betty laugh.

"I don't think she went with him willingly," Betty replied as she caught her breath.

Lillian shrugged again, clearly having no sympathy for a girl who would run to a waiting car without first considering the consequences. "She clearly knew him Bets. She went running out there and now they're gone. I say good riddance."

"That's what I say too." But Betty wasn't convinced. It didn't look like bad trash. It looked more like bad blood.

Chapter Nine

The collection of notes over Nora's desk was beginning to grow, taking up nearly every inch of available space. It was the most notes she had ever accumulated in the beginning stages of a project. She shook her head. She had to stop thinking of this as a project. It was more like...a curiosity, or, at this point, an obsession. Dave was still working on tracking down more information on Lillian's death and he hadn't even started searching for Celia Graves yet, but Nora had a feeling he was going to find something similar. She was becoming convinced that there was more than just a passing connection between Lillian and Celia, more than just a scream overheard in the night.

In the meantime, she wanted to do some digging on the girls' families. She had both their names and could approximate their dates of birth which was enough to do a cursory search through *Ancestry*. com's databases. She decided to start with Lillian since she also had her parents' names which would make it easier to assemble a family tree of sorts. Bringing up a new screen, Nora added Lillian first, then her father William and her mother Angela. Immediately a little green leaf appeared at the corner of each of the three boxes which meant there were documents that matched each family member.

She clicked on the leaf next to Lillian's box and waited for the results to load of which there were multiple pages. The first one was a record of Lillian's birth in Springfield in 1932. The second was a scan of her Elms College yearbook photo. Nothing Nora hadn't already seen but she jotted down some notes anyway before moving on to the record of her death in 1954, just after her 22nd birthday. Despite her overwhelming desire to dig into this mystery, the thought of someone dying so young depressed Nora. The next few records belonged to a Lillian Hanlon, not Hanley. *Ancestry*'s search features usually generated very generalized results so the name match wasn't always exact but as she scrolled down she found one final entry for the correct Lillian: a *Find A Grave* index entry that listed Lillian's resting place as the Springfield Cemetery on Pine Street. Nora wrote down the plot number, then pulled up a map of the cemetery.

It was the prettiest cemetery in the city, nestled between massive blocks of apartment buildings and busy streets. The cemetery somehow managed to be peaceful and quiet despite its location and its design resembled a rambling rural cemetery rather than an inner city cemetery in a less than desirable neighborhood. It was a place Nora knew well-- the cemetery in Charlie Donahue's neighborhood was based on this one. She would definitely go out to see where Lillian was buried but for now, she was focused on research.

Navigating away from the Hanley family tree, Nora opened a new window and started a new tree with Celia Graves as the only branch. She guessed that Celia, a first year in 1953, would have been born in 1935 or thereabouts. She wished she had some information about her parents but unfortunately her name and birth year were all she had to work with. Surprisingly, a leaf appeared right above Celia's name. Maybe there was something there after all.

Nora began to sift through the records, most of which she discarded based on age or location. There was a Celia Graves that was born in 1809. That certainly wasn't her. And there was a Celia Graves who was born in 1934-- close enough- but was from California. Elms certainly attracted students from all across the United States but Nora remembered the article mentioned that Celia was from West Springfield so the California Celia was also taken out of the running. But then, towards the end of the document list, there was a birth record from 1935 with the place of birth listed as Springfield, which was typical in the area as the closest major hospitals were both across the bridge from where Celia grew up. It listed her parents as Howard and Virginia Graves. Nora added the information to the newly created tree and waited to see if that generated any more specific results. If it was the correct Celia, more records should pop up.

She refreshed her screen and clicked on the green leaf that now returned far fewer but much more specific results. That was definitely the right information for Celia's parents. Records indicated that they had lived on Beauview Terrace in West Springfield. Nora looked up the address and found a charming little house that resembled a Swiss Chalet with an A-frame front door and a sloping roof line.

"Oh! Jackpot!" The Google search had returned results for the address that included the names of the current occupants: Patrick and Rebecca Graves. Relatives? Did she have a brother? Or maybe it was a cousin? Either way, it was worth checking out. She went back to the documents list and scrolled through until she found something she didn't expect: a death record.

She opened the document just as her phone rang. Dave. Nora picked up the phone without saying hello. "Celia Graves is dead."

"Yeah. How did you know?"

"I found the record of her death on *Ancestry*. It says she died in September 1953. Just days after she was last seen getting into some guy's car."

"You got it. Parents reported her missing the next day when her roommate told the RA that Celia never made it back from Elms Night. Cops investigated but no one could describe the car or the guy driving it." A phone started to ring in the background and Dave told Nora to hang on a minute.

There was a commotion on the other end of the line as Dave picked up his desk phone. Nora couldn't hear what he was saying, just heard his tone switch quickly to a much more professional one. She waited, tapping her pen on the edge of her notebook, hoping Dave would be able to give her some of the details of that investigation.

"Sorry about that. I'm the only one here right now."

"No problem," Nora replied. "So what happened with this investigation?"

"The report says they looked for her for two days until someone reported a body behind United States Rubber, you know, the old Uniroyal factory."

Nora knew the spot well. Her father had worked at Uniroyal back in the 70s but the plant was closed by 1981 after Uniroyal was bought out by Michelin. While Dave was talking Nora was searching for photos of what the plant looked like in 1953.

"It appeared that she had been dumped there, probably the same night she disappeared. She'd been strangled."

The report said there was a good deal of damage to her body but there was no way of knowing if it was from her attacker or from being left out in the elements, left out for the animals. She fought back, of that they were certain. There was a good deal of skin under her fingernails but it was 1953. DNA testing hadn't even been imagined yet. Samples were collected and preserved but Nora knew they would have degraded substantially by now and likely wouldn't produce results even if someone was to test them. Besides, she was getting way ahead of herself-- so far there was no reason to even think about reopening the case and testing anything. It was just her, a writer, letting her imagination go for a walk. Finding something that might not even be there.

"So now you've got two girls from the same college, both dead under less than typical circumstances. The only person to see Celia Graves leave that night was Lillian Hanley, and just a few months later she ends up dead too." Dave's voice had gone up in pitch and Nora could tell he too was letting his wheels turn, seeing the same connection Nora had. "I think you might have found something after all Phillips."

Nora stuck her pen in her mouth and bit down on the cap until she heard it crack. "But the question is, do I really want to know what?"

⚜

That afternoon, after collecting her thoughts and making even more notes, Nora sat down to write an email to Eric. She hadn't checked in with him for days and while that was generally normal for their working relationship, she didn't want to make him angry when he was busy protecting her from losing her advance.

To: eric.silva@greenmountainediting.com
From: Nora.Phillips1028@gmail.com

Subject: Not Dead

Eric-
Sorry for the radio silence the last couple days. I haven't forgotten our last conversation and I wanted you to know that I'm working on it. I think I might have found something I can use. Not sure yet but I'll keep you posted.
-Nora

It wasn't a lie exactly. Maybe Nora did have something, and maybe she didn't. But she had already spent time fitting Charlie Donahue into this mystery and with a few minor tweaks here and there, this would be a perfect plot for Charlie to unravel. Her email dinged and there was a return email from Eric that just said "Sounds good". He was definitely mad but at this point, he would just have to trust Nora to do her job like she always did.

Her inbox lit up again with an email from Jacqueline asking if she wanted to have lunch on campus tomorrow. She hesitated, but then thought it might make sense to talk with someone other than Selena about what they had found. She emailed Jacqueline back and accepted her invite, then headed downstairs to figure out what to feed her miserably growling stomach. She hadn't eaten anything yet; she had been running on caffeine and nothing else since she woke up and now she was beginning to develop one hell of a headache.

As she moved around the kitchen gathering together what little she could find in the way of food, her phone lit up with a text from Dave saying he would drop off copies of the reports for Nora to look through for herself. She decided to make herself a grilled cheese sandwich and a bowl of tomato soup, the ultimate comfort food on the grayest days of winter. After feeding both the animals, Nora grabbed an ice pack and put her feet up, massaging her aching knee with her fingers while Agatha Christie's Marple played in the background.

Moments later Nora heard the telltale squeak of the screen door just as she finished her dinner and Dave knocked heavily on the front door. Sliding the ice from her knee, Nora limped to the door and opened it, ushering Dave into the living room. "You want a beer?"

He waved off her offer and lowered himself into the club chair farthest from the TV that Nora clicked off as she settled back on the couch with her leg up on a stack of pillows. Dave tossed a manila folder on the coffee table and folded his hands in his lap as Nora leaned forward to pick it up.

"There's not a whole lot more in there than what I told you already but maybe there's something in there I'm not seeing that you will. I know how your brain works.

Dave knew her too well. Nora's brain did indeed work in strange ways, especially when she had a hold on an idea like this one. There were times when she was able to ferret out details that no one else noticed, dig up connections that no one else caught. She got so immersed in researching the actual cases that fed her fictional ones and that singlemindedness paid off more often than not.

"I met with one of Lillian Hanley's former classmates."

Dave said nothing but was clearly waiting for Nora to continue.

"She remembers seeing one of the nuns pulling Celia Graves aside at Elms Night just before she took off out the front door."

"Did she hear what was said?"

Nora shook her head. "No, she was up on the balcony with the other seniors but she said whatever they were talking about was enough to drive Celia out the door." She relayed to Dave what Betty had said about following Lillian around to the front of the building just in time to hear Celia scream. "So now that's two people who heard her scream."

"Two people who heard a scream that might have been Celia Graves but they can't be sure," Dave reminded her. "And neither of those people could describe the car and neither of them got a license plate."

"True. But I still think there's something there." Nora eased her frozen knee off the pillows and bent it gingerly, then stood up to stretch. "If there are now two people who heard that scream, maybe there's also someone out there who actually saw something important, something that could open this thing up."

"And how are you going to find that person? Celia Graves has been dead for decades."

Nora stood up and paced, her brow furrowed and her fists

clenched in concentration. "Well, I'm obviously going to start with tracking down the nun who talked to Celia. I know Sister Eleanor was there that night and she's still at the college. In fact, I just talked to her the other day about Lillian." Nora stopped short. "I'll actually be surprised if she didn't see the encounter with Celia."

Other than the few people left on campus, Nora was at a bit of a loss. Normally she would just start knocking on doors but the neighborhood around the college had changed a good deal since 1953. Most of the houses on Gaylord Street now belonged to the college and of course the houses on Springfield Street had changed hands multiple times in the intervening years. That would mean an extensive records search first to figure out who owned those houses in 1953, and second to track those people down.

"I'll figure it out. It might take some time, but I'll figure it out."

"I'm sure you will. Ok I'm going to leave you to it. And if anyone asks," he said, pointing to the folder. "You didn't get any of that from me."

"As always." Nora saw him to the door and watched as he climbed into his car and pulled out of her driveway. She closed and locked the door, then headed to the kitchen. Weeding through all this information was going to necessitate wine, and lots of it. She grabbed the folder and carried it, along with a large glass of wine, up to her office where the heat had settled comfortably in the room, Hank already stretched out on his pillow, fast asleep. Nora turned on her desk lamp along with the tall metal floor lamp in the corner that her mother had given her, casting a cozy glow over the room and throwing shadows across Nora's notes, some of which were already beginning to curl at the edges.

She took the photocopied records out of their folder and spread them across her desk. The first thing she wanted to do was create a timeline of events starting with Elms Night on Sunday, September 13,

1953. She marked it on the timeline and made a note to find out what time the entire ceremony would have started and when the first years would have entered the Rotunda. It would probably be helpful too if she could find out what order they did things in that year as far as the benediction, the speeches, and the singing. The singing was most important because Betty mentioned that the seniors were in the middle of their song when the unidentified nun grabbed Celia's arm to talk to her, so she marked that on the timeline with a question mark for the specific time.

The next event marked on the timeline was Celia leaving Berchmans, which happened shortly after her conversation with the nun. Nora figured that if Lillian did indeed notice Celia leaving at the exact moment she disappeared out the front door that it would have taken Lillian roughly seven minutes to make it down the back stairs and out the side door where she witnessed Celia getting into the car, presumably on Gaylord Street if Betty's account was the be trusted. At about the same time Lillian was watching Celia get into the car, Betty was also heading down the back stairwell. As she exited the side doors, Lillian had already arrived at the front doors— mere minutes before Betty rounded the corner to the front of the building— just enough time for Lillian to shut the doors as the car rounded the corner.

Nora added the car itself to the timeline, noting that as Lillian was closing the doors the car was speeding around the corner and up onto the curb. There was something about the way Betty had described that part of the evening that made Nora think that things inside the car weren't going quite as well as Celia had expected. It sounded to her like the driver was trying to make a quick getaway and had lost control of the car. Was it perhaps because Celia had changed her mind and wanted out of the car? Did he pull her back and that was why she screamed? Or had she simply screamed because she thought the car was going to crash? Nora noted all those possibilities under the car's entry on the timeline.

Then there was the gap in time between Elms Night and the discovery of Celia's body. Here, Nora would have to do a great deal of digging to fill in the blanks. Had anyone seen the car clearly enough to describe it? Where had the car gone after it was out of sight of the Elms campus? Why did it take so long for Celia to be reported missing? Nora thought it rather strange that no one was out searching for her, that instead her body had been found by an employee at United States Rubber and, judging by the paperwork Dave had given her, it took at least another day to identify her and track down her parents.

After the discovery of Celia's body, the next entry on the timeline was the day Betty saw Lillian alive for the very last time. Nora marked their breakfast on the timeline, followed by the custodian discovering Lillian passed out in a classroom. Next came the infirmary visit which occurred at nearly midnight according to the nurse's report from that night. Lillian was pronounced dead shortly after and her body transported to the hospital.

Nora sat back and looked at the timeline. The timeline that resembled a piece of Swiss cheese for all the holes. That was a lot of time unaccounted for and Nora knew she would have to fill those in if she was going to find a real connection between the two girls. She opened her laptop and pulled up a map of Springfield Street and its surrounding neighborhoods, found the clearest one in the search results, and sent it to print. It wasn't likely that there would be any kind of neighborhood map online from 1953; for that she would have to go to the archives. Then she would be able to cross reference properties and try to trace the previous owners.

The houses on Gaylord Street might prove a bit easier. The purchase and sale records were likely housed somewhere at the College and that would at least give Nora the names of the most recent owners who had sold out to the college. With any luck, those names wouldn't be too far removed from the original families. Thankfully back in the day, families tended to stay in those neighborhoods as long as they could. The area around the college was primarily Polish and the community was anchored by Holy Name Church.

The other thing she wanted to do was drive through Celia's old neighborhood in West Springfield, see if there was anyone left who remembered the family, figure out who Patrick and Rebecca were. Nora wanted to get a better sense of Celia, beyond being just another young girl who got into the wrong car. She also wanted to see if she could find where Celia was buried. There hadn't been any record on Ancestry like there was for Lillian but that information had to be somewhere. It was unlikely that either girls' parents were still alive but maybe a bit more digging would unearth a sibling or even a distant cousin.

Feeling like she had at least accomplished something, Nora put her pen down and her laptop to sleep, her own brain feeling like it was time for a power down. She swallowed the last sip of wine in her glass, the rest of which she didn't even remember drinking, and turned off the lights before she headed downstairs. She didn't have the energy to clean up her dinner dishes so she left them for the morning and just barely got her pajamas on before her eyelids began to droop. She climbed under the blankets and rolled over to cuddle Luna who had already made herself comfortable on Nora's fur lined comforter.

CHAPTER TEN

When she woke the next morning it had snowed again, a light dusting that covered the grass and the very tips of the tree branches. It was soft, clean snow that sparkled in the sun and made Nora want to stay inside with a good book and a cup of hot tea, but instead she was bundled up in jeans, boots, and a heavy sweater under her down coat, waiting for her car to warm up. Hank and Luna were cuddled up together in the massive dog bed she had had to buy so they could both fit in it. Hank opened one sleepy eye and looked up at her as if to say, *Why in the world are you going outside in that?* He was not a fan of snow. Or the cold. Or of being awake for more than twenty minutes at a time.

The streets were wet and traffic was light as Nora headed for Beauview Terrace and Celia Graves' old house, number fifty six. There was a car in the driveway and it looked like someone was home. Nora pulled up to the curb and grabbed her bag, notebook, and pen. She knocked on the front door and stepped back while she waited for someone to answer it, surprised to see that it was a man about her own age who opened the door.

"Can I help you?" He asked, his brow furrowed.

"I'm hoping you can. I'm Nora Phillips. I'm a writer." She waved her notebook as if that cemented her place as an author. "Anyway," she cleared her throat, "I'm looking for information on a family that lived here back in the early 1950s."

He stared at her for a moment, his blue eyes narrowed in either suspicion or deep thought, Nora couldn't tell which. His blond hair was combed neatly away from his face and he was wearing a long sleeved shirt that looked rather expensive. His dark wash jeans looked like they had quite possibly been pressed. "Do you mean the Graves family?"

"Yes. Do you know them?"

"I do. They're relatives of mine."

Nora breathed a sigh of relief. Maybe this was going to be easier than she thought. "I was hoping I could speak with someone about Celia Graves."

He made a sound that was part derisive snort, part choking noise. "Of course you are. So you're not a writer, you're a reporter." He shook his head. "We've told every single one of you who has managed to find this house that we're not interested in telling you anything. My great aunt is dead and gone, her case is closed." With that he slammed the door shut and Nora heard the deadbolt turn.

Great aunt. That means Celia Graves had at least one sibling. Was there a chance she had more? Nora got in her car and started the engine, giving it a minute or two to warm up again. She fiddled with the radio for a moment until she was startled by a sudden, sharp rap on her window. Nora looked up to find an older woman— late 50s, early 60s– waiting for her to roll down the window.

"Can I help you?"

"I just wanted to apologize for my son's rudeness," she said as she stamped her feet and rubbed her arms to ward off the cold. "He's very protective of my Aunt Celia even though he never met her." She stuck her hand through the window and Nora shook it carefully. "I'm Alice."

"It's fine. I'm used to having doors slammed in my face."

"I'm so sorry. Steven thought you were a reporter but I recognized you from the photo on the back of your books." Alice smiled. "I love your Charlie Donahue series."

Nora returned her smile. "Thank you so much."

"Are you thinking of using Celia's story in one of your books?"

Nora had no idea how to answer that. Was she? And if she was, what would this woman, Celia's niece, think of that idea? She decided to go with honesty. "I don't know actually. I came across your aunt's murder along with the death of another student that seemed suspicious. I just wanted to see if there was a connection."

"You mean Lillian Hanley?"

She nodded.

"Of course there's a connection."

Nora found herself in Alice's tiny kitchen while her son hovered nervously in the doorway. Alice was making tea, bustling around while Steven's eyes bored into the back of Nora's neck but she refused to give him the satisfaction of turning to look at him. Instead she kept her eyes on Alice, pretending Steven wasn't there, glaring at her.

"There you go dear." Alice set a mug of tea in front of Nora and pushed a sugar dish and creamer towards her. "Unless you prefer lemon?"

"No, milk and sugar is just fine, thank you."

Alice took a breath, then wrapped her hands around her teacup to warm them up. "My Aunt Celia was less of an aunt and more like a cousin. There was quite an age gap between her and my father so when I was born in 1946 she was only a teenager. She used to babysit me. Until she went away to college that is."

"What was she like?"

"She was fun. Lots of fun. She always had some kind of little gift for me when she babysat. Sometimes she came to our house but usually my father dropped me off here, my grandparents' house. I have a lot of very fond memories in this house." She looked around as if she was seeing some of them play out as she talked. "When my grandparents passed they left the house to my father. Then it came to me."

Nora had always loved this particular house and she told Alice so. When she was young and rented her first apartment it was in a converted Victorian house just up the hill on Witch Path, across from the cemetery. It was where she was living when the first Charlie Donahue mystery was born. In fact, the church in Charlie's town was modeled after the former Masonic lodge that Nora could see from her front yard.

Alice had been close to her Aunt Celia and her murder had hit hard. Her father retreated into himself after the loss of his younger sister and life was never the same for Alice's family. For months after Celia's body was found the house was surrounded by reporters while the police came in and out, asking a million questions about Celia's life, her friends, her behavior prior to her disappearance. Of course, no one could really answer those questions since Celia had moved into O'Leary Hall weeks before she was taken away. Her family had no idea who might have been in that car; they had no knowledge of any boyfriends or any other relationships that may have gone bad.

Celia's few hometown friends had quickly lost touch with her when she left for Elms, as happened frequently when girls went away to school. She may have only been twenty minutes away, but for her childhood friends, it might as well have been another world. The moment Celia put on her Elms blazer, she was an Elms girl and little else. That was why her family found it so puzzling that she was willing to get in that car with someone they assumed was a complete stranger.

"No one had a clue who he was or where he had come from," Alice said with a shrug. "We couldn't fathom how he had found Celia, where they had met, since the girls rarely left campus, especially in the first few weeks of school. The nuns rarely let the girls out of their sight."

"Alice, someone said that just before Celia got in that car one of the nuns had pulled her aside, said something to her that seemed to trigger her leaving. Do you know anything about that?"

Alice shook her head slowly. "She used to mention one of the nuns, someone she got along with fairly well but I can't remember her name. Celia told me about her. Sometimes I wish Celia had been more of a letter writer so I could remember better."

She might not have been a letter writer but she was still a young girl. Nora wondered aloud if perhaps Celia had kept a diary?

"I don't think so," Alice said. "At least there wasn't one in her belongings when they cleared out her room."

"Do you happen to remember which room was hers?"

Alice thought for a moment, then tapped her index finger on the table. "I think it was on the third floor. I remember the ceilings were rather low, sharp angles. It was tucked away in a little hallway that I thought was cozy but I only got to see it once. My father took me to visit when Celia first moved in."

That description sounded an awful lot like Selena's room. Nora made a quick note in her book about the room, though the odds were slim that anything had been left behind given that the room had had many inhabitants since Celia's time there. It was highly unlikely that there was any sign of Celia left there but it wouldn't hurt to take a closer look around.

Nora was silent for a moment, considering what Alice had told her even though, on the surface it was very little. She still had no more information about Celia's death than she had before but at least now she felt she might know her just a little bit better. "Thank you so much for all of this Alice. I can't tell you how much I appreciate you talking with me."

"Of course. I hope that, in the end, you can learn at least a little bit about what happened to my aunt. The police have left the case open as they never did find who did it, but we all know it's gone cold, it's no longer an active case. And it'll stay that way unless someone can find new information."

Alice was looking at her as if she believed Nora might be that someone. There was so much sadness in her eyes when she talked about Celia but there was also a spark of hope, one that grew as she talked about Nora's interest in the case.

"I'll do my best Alice. If I find anything you'll certainly be the first to know." Nora waited as Alice scrawled her phone number on a piece of paper that had teddy bears and butterflies printed in the margins. It was the kind of paper Nora's mother used to write her shopping lists on.

She thanked Alice again, slipping the paper into her notebook where she knew she would be able to find it again should she need it. When she stood, Alice did as well and reached out to gather Nora into her arms and hugged her tightly. "I'm just grateful that not everyone has forgotten Celia."

Nora walked out of the house with a smile on her face but also the nagging thought that there was now a great deal of pressure on her to find something that would put Celia's case back on the front burner for police. As she picked her way down the walk to her car, Nora looked over her shoulder to find Alice's son, Steven, watching her from the living room window. His expression was nearly impossible to read but Nora guessed that he wasn't happy about all the information his mother had shared with her but the moment he caught Nora's eye he stepped back and let the curtains fall, obscuring her view into the house. It was just as well. She had gotten all she needed.

CHAPTER ELEVEN

An hour later she was pulling into the lot at Elms for her lunch date with Jacqueline. She had been minutes away from canceling but she knew that she needed a sounding board that wasn't Selena. Her visit with Alice cemented that need. She parked in the student lot behind the dorms, hoping that her graduate school parking sticker would be enough to keep her from getting ticketed since she was in too much of a rush to walk all the way from the circle on the other side of Berchmans. Jacqueline had already gotten a table in the dining hall and was sitting comfortably with a dog-eared novel propped open on the table. There was a bit of a line snaking its way out of the kitchen, which likely explained why Jacqueline didn't seem concerned about picking up a tray at that moment.

"Hey. Sorry I'm late."

Jacqueline looked down at her watch and frowned. "You're literally two minutes late. If that."

"It felt like longer. I've been rushing around since the crack of dawn."

"Oh. Intrigue. Tell me more."

Nora dropped her bag on the table and took her coat off, slinging it over the empty chair next to her. "Where to even begin…" Pulling out the timeline she had written, Nora filled Jacqueline in on things as far as she'd gotten with things. "There are just so many missing pieces."

"But you think there's something there?"

"I do. I'm just not sure what yet. I met Celia's niece, Alice who said she wasn't sure if her aunt used to keep a journal but in the mother of all coincidences, I think Selena now lives in Celia's old room. I'm wondering if maybe she did keep a journal– like all girls her age– and it's just hidden somewhere the police never would have thought to look."

Jacqueline eyed the lunch line as it died down, then waved Nora over to grab a tray. She chatted as they moved through the cafeteria, adding things to her plate as she went. "It sounds like you found some inspiration here after all."

"Oh god no." Shaking her head, Nora grabbed a plate of chicken and green beans onto her tray. "I'm just distracting myself honestly."

"Ah, I see. So this isn't you breaking your writer's block?"

"Definitely not. That's not what this is." Or was it? Was this a distraction or plotting? Was her timeline helping to solve the crime or helping her outline her next book? She wanted to deny it, but her furious writing the other night was telling her otherwise. Obviously, she had written all that down just to write something, just to get something down on paper but maybe it was more than that. "I don't know. I'm not sure what to do with all this. Besides, this is Selena's wheelhouse. She started it all."

"No, she tried to pull you into her nutbag conspiracy theory," Jacqueline replied with a laugh as she filled a cloudy plastic cup with Diet Coke. "And now you've stumbled on something far bigger. At this point, I don't think Selena even factors into this anymore."

If only she knew that the moment Nora was done eating she was planning to break into Selena's room. Selena was a bigger part of this whole thing than she even knew. And Nora wasn't about to tell her either, a fact that scared her a little. She was already thinking of this as her investigation, her story to follow. She was already thinking of how she could turn this to her advantage, a thought that sickened her if she was being honest with herself.

"I feel like I owe her something for having shown me the newspapers to begin with."

"Nora, she dragged you down into the basement of your old college dorm and showed you some musty newspapers. Which, by the way, she only showed you because you pretended to be interested in her theories about some decades-old scandal."

"Which just happened to be true, Jacqueline." Although, at the same time, her former professor had a point. Selena may have noticed the line items, but it was Nora's connections that had fleshed out the tale. Nora followed Jacqueline back to the table and set her tray down. "I guess you're right. I mean, it's not like I'm stepping on her toes or anything."

"How would you, the New York Times Bestselling author, ever step on the toes of a first year undergrad who doesn't know her elbow from a hole in the ground?"

Laughing, Nora sat down and pulled her chair in, picking up her fork. "You're right. I guess if I decided to write about this there's nothing stopping me."

"Exactly. So you're going to write about it."

"That's not what I said, Jacqueline." But Nora realized that that was exactly what she meant, that this was just what she needed to get out of her rut. She finished off her dinner and glanced at her watch. It was time to get over to O'Leary and see if she could find something that would make all this back and forth worth it.

Nora left Jacqueline and made it to the front of O'Leary Hall just as an unsuspecting undergrad opened the door, allowing Nora to slip in behind her. Thankfully there was no one manning the desk so she didn't have to worry about having someone sign her in. Or having any evidence that she was even there.

She took the stairs two at a time all the way to the third floor where she hoped Selena had been stupid enough to leave her door unlocked. Nora came to the alcove where Selena's room was and waited to see if she could hear anything from inside but all appeared quiet. Creeping slowly up to the door, Nora reached out and tried the knob.

"Hallelujah," she whispered, the knob turning easily in her hand. That likely meant Selena had just stepped out for a moment so Nora had to be quick. Of course the greatest problem at hand was that she had no idea what it was she was looking for. Celia's initials scratched into a desktop perhaps? Or maybe some discarded piece of something that had gotten wedged in somewhere for all eternity. She shook her head, clearing it of those kinds of fanciful thoughts. Odds were slim she would find anything at all but she had to satisfy her curiosity.

Nora began to paw carefully through Selena's room, running her fingers over the top of her desk-- clean by the way- looking under the bed and in the wardrobe. If she was a young woman in the early 1950s, keeping a diary she wouldn't want her roommate to snoop through, where would she keep it? Nora looked around the room for any nooks or warrens where something like a journal might be kept but there was nothing obvious. Nothing as Nora made her way around the room, testing every corner, every edge, until she found a floorboard that didn't quite fit.

"Can't be," she breathed. "God what a cliché."

Nora dug her heel into the end of the floorboard and watched as the other flipped up, revealing a space beneath. In that space was a small leatherbound book tied shut with a ribbon. She reached down and gently lifted the book from its hiding place and turned it over in her hands to find Celia's name embossed on the cover. Finally. A real break.

As she headed for the door, Nora turned and surveyed the room, making sure she hadn't left a thing out of place. It seemed too good to be true that finding Celia's journal had been that easy and the last thing she needed was to complicate it by getting caught snooping. She opened the door a crack and listened for footsteps or voices in the hallway but it still appeared to be empty so Nora took her leave, pulling Selen's door shut behind her.

Nora headed down the stairs to the first floor but instead of walking immediately out to her car she decided to take a quick detour to the basement where she found herself under the staircase, pushing on the door to "The Study". The door was swollen and stuck on its hinges; Nora had to apply all her body weight to get it to budge even the smallest bit. She considered putting her shoulder to the door but then thought better of it since that would likely lead to quite a bruise and she didn't need any more bodily injuries. Instead, she leaned in and put considerable force into her hip, shoving at the door until it opened just enough for her to squeeze through.

Surprisingly the lights still worked, the sconces just barely illuminating the room with the flip of the switch. Nora looked around and found that the room had not changed at all since her time there. It was almost like walking into the past— her past that is. She almost expected Margaret to be curled up on that horrid green couch with a bowl of microwave popcorn and a book, but all that greeted her was dust motes floating lazily in the tepid pools of yellow light.

The billiards table looked a little worse for wear and when Nora peered into the pockets she found that the billiard balls were gone along with the one cue that she and Margaret used to share. Everything else remained the same, including the layers of dust on nearly every surface. This seemed the perfect place to read through Celia's journal.

Had the green couch been that dirty when she and Margaret used to lounge on it? Massive clouds of dust rose from the cushions as Nora beat at them with the palm of her hand, trying to make a somewhat acceptable place to sit but the filth was overwhelming. It was a losing battle, one Nora surrendered to quickly, settling herself in the very corner of the couch and putting its less-than-desirable state of cleanliness out of her mind. All that mattered was that the room was as warm as she remembered it and she would be left alone in here for as long as she liked.

Opening the journal felt something like the climax of a hero's quest. She had the magic item and untying the ribbon from around the pages would release its powers. In this case, its power to potentially answer a great number of questions. Nora knew that if she found anything in this journal she would have to turn it in to the police. At the very least she should hand it over to Alice should she discover that there wasn't any evidence in there at all, just the angst ridden ramblings of a teenage girl. Either way, she wanted time to move slowly through the journal so that when she got home she could photocopy whatever she felt was pertinent before losing custody of the book.

On the inside flap of the journal was an inscription: "To Celia. Happy birthday and best wishes in your senior year! Love, Mother". Below that Celia had written her full name and the date, August 17, 1952. On the next page she had very carefully written her address and phone number on the off chance that the journal was ever misplaced. Nora was sure Celia never imagined a mystery writer, a stranger, reading her words fifty years later. She certainly never imagined she'd be long dead by the time her journal was found.

Nora leafed through the pages quickly, skimming entries about the first day of senior year, her first failed exam, the last first dance that she would ever have as a high school student. It wasn't that Nora wasn't interested in Celia's life before Elms, it was just that she preferred to fast-forward to the important bits, the ones that might tell her who was in that car. She moved ahead to the entries that started after she moved into O'Leary Hall. Celia went into painstaking detail about her room which she seemed to be very enamored of. It gave Nora goosebumps to read about Celia living in the same room she had, describing the same desk Nora had sat at, the same chair, the same wardrobe. She even mentioned finding a good hiding place for her journal as she had been promised a roommate who hadn't yet arrived and she certainly didn't want some strange girl pawing through her book which made Nora feel guilty for intruding on her private thoughts, but it couldn't be helped. One of the early entries about her new experience at Elms gave Nora a good laugh:

September 7, 1953

> *Today was orientation for the first years. We met our big sisters and took yet another tour of the campus. Of course the upperclassmen took us up to the fourth floor of Berchmans and told us that ridiculous story about the girl who killed herself. My friend Gwen's older sister said they would do that. She knows because she went to Elms too. She said they do it just to scare the first years which is just hazing if you ask me. But I do love the view from the fourth floor right into the reading room of the library. It's such a beautiful, soaring space with stacks and stacks of books. It looks like the perfect place to study.*

It was sad to think Celia never got a chance to study in that library, or anywhere else for that matter, but on the other hand Nora found it funny that Celia wasn't at all impressed by the Catherine legend. She went on to describe some of the classrooms, her favorite being one of the smallest rooms in Berchmans on the first floor. "Right near the Bursar's office!" Nora said aloud, easily recognizing the classroom Celia was describing. It was where Nora's French class was her first semester at Elms. The room was so small there were only two rows of desks and the front row was literally at the professor's feet but it was the perfect classroom to have during winter when the heat came on and steam hissed through the small space, warming fingers and toes that had been sacrificed to the cold on the walk over from the dorms.

There weren't many entries to go through before Nora came to the morning of Elms Night and she worried that the journal wouldn't yield anything useful but then she started reading the entry from that day.

September 13, 1953
Elms Night is tonight and I can't wait to get my beanie.
I already have my blazer and I pressed it specially for
tonight. We've been preparing our class song and I think
the seniors will be quite impressed. This morning I walked
down to the corner store with Evelyn for a bottle of Coke
and the strangest thing happened. Halfway down Spring-
field Street a car slowed down, a black one with a man
driving it. He had his passenger window rolled down and
he shouted to us from the car.

Blowing out a frustrated sigh, Nora turned the journal over and balanced it on her knee, keeping her place at the back of it. After that entry, of course, the book was blank and though Celia did indeed come in contact with this car before that final moment, there still didn't seem to be any clues as to why she would have left the campus with him. She went to pick up the book again and an envelope fluttered out from between the pages and landed on the floor. Nora bent to pick it up and slid out a piece of composition paper folded in fours, carefully creased. As she unfolded it, she took in the sharp, pointed handwriting that appeared rushed and agitated. Glancing over what appeared to be a letter addressed to Celia, Nora noticed places where the writer had pushed so hard on the pencil point that it had gone right through. The letter wasn't dated. The postmark only said the year and was canceled in Springfield. No return address.

Dearest Celia-

Have you gotten any of my other letters? I hope you have and just haven't had time to respond. I know a college girl like you is probably busy but you should have written back by now. Why haven't you written? Do you not remember me? I thought I had given you enough to remember me by in my last letter.

Celia, if you don't write me back soon and put me out of my misery, I'm going to have to come there, to the college, and find you. Don't you understand I'm in love with you? I don't know how many times I have to say it to you. Just please respond.

Yours,

Joel

Was this the man in the car? Did Joel follow through on his promise to come to the college and find her? Folding the note back up, Nora slid it back into its envelope and tucked it into the front cover of the journal which she then hid in the back pocket of her bag, the pocket with the Velcro so it couldn't accidentally fall out. She took the stairs two at a time and made a break for the front door, past the RA that was now manning the front desk, brushing past a group of students, the girls from Jacqueline's class, who stared after her, bewildered.

"Wasn't that that author?" One girl asked.

Another shrugged. "She's a train wreck."

They laughed and let the door close behind them but Nora didn't hear any of that because she was already halfway to her car. She slammed her door and jammed her key in the ignition, then jerked the car into drive. Hooking a quick right out of the lot and a left onto Gaylord Street, Nora suddenly pictured Joel in his black car doing the same, rushing towards the stop sign at the intersection with Springfield Street. But Nora went right instead of left, heading for the highway, heading for home.

She angled her car into her driveway and barely got her bag onto her shoulder before she was out of the car and heading for the front door. Nora didn't even take off her coat when she got inside, just ran upstairs to her office and pulled out her timeline with all her notes. Digging for a pen, Nora added "Joel— black car" under the entry for Celia's disappearance. Did she know this guy Joel? Had she actually seen all his letters and that was why she got in his car that night? Or did she just want to get away for some reason?

The moment she finished writing his name on the timeline Nora knew what she had to do: she had to turn the book over to the police. It certainly wasn't a smoking gun by any means but it was something. Something more than the nothing they had to go on before. Maybe Celia's parents would know who Joel was. But first, she had to call Dave.

CHAPTER TWELVE

For the second time in as many days Nora found herself perched on a barstool next to Dave as he leafed through Celia's journal. Before she got there Nora had pulled the letter out and held it to the side while Dave read; Nora had already reread the entire thing to make sure there was no other mention of Joel and his letters but there was nothing. When he got to the final entry, he went back to the beginning and very carefully paged through it a second time. He flattened the book out on the bar and bent down so that he was at eye level with the spine, running his finger along the inside edge of the pages.

"What are you doing?"

He stood up straight and gestured at the book. "There are pages missing."

"What?" Nora pushed Dave out of the way and bent down to see what he had found. There were tiny little jagged edges sticking up from the stitching in the book's binding. He was right. Someone had torn out some of the pages. "I'll be damned. I didn't even notice that. This was in the back by the way, tucked into that flap." She handed him the letter and watched him read it, then check the postmark exactly as she had done.

"My guess is whoever ripped the pages out missed the letter. Looks like there was plenty in there that someone didn't want getting out."

"So you think those pages could have something to do with this Joel guy?"

Dave shrugged. "That's my best guess at this point. He clearly

116

sent her more than just that one letter so it stands to reason she would have mentioned him in the diary."

"Yet she didn't recognize him when he called out to her from his car."

"Maybe he was delusional," Dave suggested. "Maybe she didn't know him at all and that's why she didn't recognize him. Or maybe they only crossed paths briefly and he blew it out of proportion. I'm wondering what happened to the other letters."

"I'm wondering the same thing." Sighing, Nora closed the book and tucked the letter back in where it belonged. "I'm going to turn this over to the Chicopee police."

"I can do that for you. I have a couple buddies on the force over there." Nora handed the journal back to Dave.

"Thanks, I appreciate it." She grabbed one of her business cards and tacked it to the front of the notebook. "Tell them they can call me any time."

She felt strange letting the journal out of her sight but she knew it was what had to be done. Even if it led nowhere, the police still needed to see what Celia had written and they certainly needed to see that letter. Besides, she had already taken photocopies of both. "Seriously, they can call me any time," she said, tapping her index finger on the bar, confident that Dave would take it from there.

As she left the bar Nora thought about what Dave had said about the other letters. Had they disappeared along with the pages from the notebook? Or was there a chance that Celia had hidden those as expertly as she'd hidden the journal? There was really only one way to find out. She needed to get back into Selena's room. She got on the highway for the second time that day and headed back to campus, parking in the exact same spot. It was already getting dark but the security guard was nowhere to be found. In Nora's case that was good news. She had gotten away without a ticket earlier and she was hoping for a repeat of that luck.

Unfortunately, there was no one headed into O'Leary, no one she could sneak in with, and the RA was on duty at the desk. She had no choice but to call Selena.

"I'm on campus. Can I come up?"

"Um, sure?" Selena sounded somewhat surprised that Nora had called her. She had given Nora her number weeks ago and this was the first time she had used it. "I'll be right down."

Nora waited on the porch, her arms wrapped around her for warmth while she stamped her feet to keep the cold from the stone platform from seeping through her boots and into her bones. A few minutes later the door opened.

"Come on in." Selena held the door open and waited for Nora to sign herself in. They climbed the stairs in silence, the hissing radiators occupying the silence instead. Inside Selena's room she pulled the desk chair out and gestured for Nora to sit while she arranged herself on a pile of pillows stacked on the floor. "What's up?"

"I need to tell you something and I'm not sure you're going to like all of what I have to say."

Selena frowned. "Ok," she replied, dragging out the syllables, filling them with doubt.

Taking a deep breath, Nora told her everything, about sneaking into her room, about finding the journal, about the letter.

"You were in my room? Without telling me?"

Nora looked away, not saying a word, her fingertips drumming against her bottom lip.

"How did you even get in here?"

With a quick raise of one eyebrow, Nora answered Selena's question.

"The door was unlocked wasn't it." Selena blew out a sigh and leaned back on her pillow pile. "I must have gone to Alexandra's room to study. I always leave my door unlocked because her room is right around the corner. I never had a reason to lock my door." She laughed, a hollow angry laugh. "Until now that is."

Nora didn't really know what to say to make what she did any more acceptable. Of course Selena would have found out eventually but now she was angry that Nora had turned it over to the police without telling her. She felt like she'd been left out and of course Nora understood that but she explained to Selena that she had to turn it over, that it was the right thing to do and Selena would have done the same had she been the one to find the diary. Selena would eventually understand that they both had a responsibility to the crime they were now researching, a duty to make sure justice was done, and if one of them had something in hand that would help achieve that, they couldn't hide it from the authorities just because they wanted it to achieve her own ends.

"That journal was in my room," Selena huffed. "Therefore it should, by rights, be mine. I should have been the one to decide what was done with it."

"No Selena," Nora sighed, shaking her head. "That journal is Celia's. It just happened to be found in your room. Now it's in the possession of the police where it belongs."

"You shouldn't have handed it over without telling me first!" Her voice was rising and Nora was grateful that she had shut the door behind them. Hopefully Selena's shouting wouldn't attract any attention.

"What's done is done Selena. I'm not going to argue semantics with you."

Selena got up off the floor and stood with her fists clenched at her sides. "You just wanted the information for yourself. For your book." She practically spat out her words. "I know you plan on writing about all this. You're going to go off and write another bestseller using all of *my* research, *my* story."

"You think that's what this is all about?" Sitting up straighter, Nora mimicked Selena's outraged pose. "You think this is all for a book? A girl was murdered, Selena. Possibly two in fact. Girls whose families have never had any kind of closure, any hope of justice. You're more immature, and far more selfish, than I realized if you truly think this is because of a book!" Nora got to her feet and faced Selena, her anger heating her cheeks, her eyes watering with frustration. "I'm glad I turned the book over without talking to you first. I thought you had it in you to do the right thing but maybe I was wrong."

Selena stuck her thumbnail in her mouth and gnawed at it until it was ragged, the nail polish flaking off and falling to the floor. Her chest rose and fell as her outrage dissipated and she considered Nora's words. "Fine, yes. The police needed to see it. And I would have turned it over, you know I would have. I just would have liked to have been in on it instead of having you go behind my back."

"You're right Selena. I shouldn't have done that." Nora sighed and sat down on the edge of the empty bed across from Selena's. "I'm not used to including anyone else in my process. I've been doing this for so long that when I get immersed in a mystery I tend to just…do what I need to do to move through the story."

"I get that," Selena admitted as she sat on her own bed, pulling a pillow into her lap. "But now you have someone else to consider. I'm just as much a part of this as you are."

Looking around the room, Nora remembered why she was here and it wasn't to argue with Selena. "There might be more hidden in here. More letters maybe."

"Wait, what?" Selena looked up at Nora, surprised, then she smirked, tenting her fingers and resting them against the tip of her nose as if she was contemplating something hilarious. "Let me guess. You actually came here to ask me to help you find them. In *my* room.

My room that you *broke into* and stole from."

Blowing out another sigh, Nora stood up and made to leave but Selena reached out and stopped her.

"You really think there's something else hidden in here?"

"I don't know. But it's worth a look." Nora looked down at Selena's hand clasped around her arm. The girl let go and muttered a nearly silent apology.

Nora returned to the spot where she had found the journal, kicking up the floorboard. She dropped her bag on the floor and fished out a tiny flashlight that she shone inside the hole left by the floorboard that she had grabbed and tossed aside. Getting down on her hands and knees, Nora tried to see if there was anything else tucked away in the blackness but it was empty. Behind her, Selena was already testing some of the other floorboards but so far they all remained stubbornly, resolutely in place.

"Where else could we look?"

Replacing the floorboard, Nora realized she shouldn't have knelt down; there was no way her knee was going to let her get back up without help. She put her right foot up and leaned heavily on her bad knee, wincing with pain.

"Are you ok?" Selena took a step forward and held her hand out to Nora. "Do you need a hand getting up?"

Nora was seeing stars, the small strikes of pain suddenly pulsing behind her kneecap. She had been so eager to find something that she had forgotten she couldn't bend like she used to. "Yeah. I forgot about my knee."

"What's wrong with it?"

"I had surgery recently. That's why I've been on campus so much." Nora took Selena's hand and took a breath, then pulled herself up. "I've been swimming to try to strengthen it but it's definitely not made for kneeling on hardwood floors anymore."

Nora rubbed her knee with her fingertips, closing her eyes as the pain faded little by little. She straightened up and took a deep breath. "Ok. I'm good. Sorry about that."

"It's ok." Selena brushed it off. "I should have gotten down there instead."

"It's fine. You didn't know." Nora looked around, trying to put herself in Celia's place, trying to think of what other hiding places she could come up with. The windows had flat trim as opposed to casings so there was nowhere to hide anything there. Nora had already searched the wardrobe, a fact she wasn't about to share with Selena, and the desk was also clean. "Baseboards?"

Selena bent and made a circuit around the room, testing the baseboards with her fingertips but nothing came loose. "Ugh. There's nowhere else in here that you could hide something!"

Nora shared her frustration but tried to keep it tamped down so she could think. "What about the alcove in the hallway? There are baseboards out there. And there's the windowsill. Maybe that can be moved?"

They both headed for the hallway, Selena making a beeline for the baseboards while Nora checked the windowsill. She was shocked when the wide wooden plank dislodged itself and slid forward, revealing a space between the wall joists, wedged against the outside and the plaster inside. Bracing the sill against her waist, Nora leaned forward and reached her hand into the first space but came up empty, and again in the next space. It was the final space, all the way to the right, where her fingers finally met with something that felt like it could be...something. "Selena, I found something. I need my flashlight."

Selena rushed over and steadied the sill while Nora fished in her pocket for her light. Leaning over as far as she could, she shined her flashlight into the space and saw what looked like a brick of papers tied together with twine. She kept her light on it while Selena reached over her and carefully extracted it. When she was sure Selena had pulled the bundle clear of the space, Nora pushed the sill back into place and followed Selena into her room, closing the door carefully behind her. Putting the bundle on the desk, Selena left the chair for Nora while she stood, her hip cocked against the corner.

"You should open them," Nora said, pushing the pile towards her. "It looks like it's more letters."

"Are you sure?" Selena was clearly excited about opening them but didn't want to step on Nora's toes, despite her earlier bluster about the journal.

"I'm sure. Go for it."

Selena carefully untied the twine, unwrapping it from the papers where it left indents on all four edges from being tied for so long. Nora could only imagine how much heat and humidity had gotten inside that open space, slowly eating away at the little packet of envelopes. Thankfully there seemed to be minimal damage, most of it to the outermost envelopes. Selena worked slowly and carefully to separate each of the envelopes before she opened the first one and unfolded the letter that was inside.

"Dear Celia," she read aloud. "I saw you today at Johnson's Bookstore downtown. I know you love books so I shouldn't be surprised."

"Wow. Was he following her?"

Selena shrugged, her eyes skimming over the rest of the letter. "He talks about seeing what she bought and how nice she looked in her yellow dress."

"What's the postmark on that one?"

Flipping over the envelope, Selena squinted at the faded date stamp. "I think it's 1953."

Nora reached out and started flipping over the other envelopes, then arranged them in date order. There were far more than she realized; they went as far back as 1951. She handed Selena the earliest one and said, "Start there and work forward. We need to get an idea of how they met."

"How do we know they even met?"

"We don't. Hopefully the letters will help us figure that out for certain." Nora paused. "I have a hunch this was something more along the lines of stalking though."

"I agree. And this first letter certainly makes it sound that way. Listen…" Selena began to read.

> *Dear Celia-*
> *I don't know if you remember me. We've met once before although there were a lot of other people around so it's understandable if you don't remember me, but I certainly remember you. I wondered if you might write me back and perhaps we can be properly introduced.*
> *Joel*

"Where's the next one?"

Nora handed Selena another, taking the first letter and carefully returning it to its envelope.

"It looks like she must have responded to his first letter. He says it's okay that she doesn't remember him; she must have apologized though it sounds to me like she wouldn't have had any reason to remember him. He says that he would like to meet her somewhere."

Nora was already opening the next letter, taking in Joel's growing desperation. "She must have said no to meeting him. He seems angry in this one, like she insulted him by saying no." She handed the letter off to Selena so she could judge for herself. "He's definitely a little off judging by this one."

"A little? This next one is even pushier. Saying he knows

where she lives and he's prepared to show up on her doorstep. What was he going to do? Negotiate with her father for an arranged marriage?"

"Don't joke," Nora laughed. "Wealthy people did that well into the 1960s. And royalty still does it."

"That's just weird."

Over the course of the next few letters Joel got increasingly intense. By the fifth letter, he was clearly stalking Celia, telling her where she had been on a given day, who she had seen, what she had bought, where she had eaten. Nora wondered if Celia had ever told anyone or if she had just assumed Joel was harmless until he wasn't.

"Ok," Selena sighed, taking the stack of letters and neatly tapping them down, winding the twine around them. "We need to turn these over too. Maybe the police will be able to find some clue in these as to who this Joel person is."

"I have no idea how, but you're right. The police need to have all the same pieces to the puzzle that we have."

Selena bit her bottom lip and looked down at the letters.

"What?" Nora asked, Selena's face pinched with worry.

"I can't believe this is real. I never thought anything would come of those news pieces, that they were just as much a legend as the Catherine story. Instead I've unwittingly unearthed a murder."

"Maybe two."

Selena's head snapped up. "What do you mean?"

"Lillian Hanley. Her death was not from any kind of illness." Nora paused, trying to decide how to put it gently. "She was poisoned."

"Do you think—"

"—it has something to do with Celia? I'm not sure. But it seems like too much of a coincidence."

"How do we find out?"

Nora sighed. "I think it's time to talk to Lillian Hanley's parents."

1953

Lillian rarely got mail. She was from the neighborhood, her parents lived only just down the street, and her closest friends had been accepted to Elms right along with her so she was suitably surprised when she was told there was a letter for her on mail day. It was in a ratty envelope that looked as if it had traveled halfway around the world before making its way to her. There was no return address and the postmark was Springfield.

"Who's it from?" Maryanne Sullivan leaned over, curious to see who might be writing her closest friend.

But Lillian only shrugged. "Don't know. There's no return address and I don't recognize the handwriting." She tilted the envelope so Maryanne could see the writing. It was messy and written in pencil. It looked as though the writer had been in a great hurry, perhaps even slightly aggravated.

"Maybe it's a secret admirer!" Maryanne teased, bumping her shoulder gently against Lillian's. Boys were always at the forefront of Maryanne's thinking, unlike Lillian who viewed dating and, in general, the opposite sex as a great distraction.

"Well, I feel bad for him if that's the case because he'll not get far here." Maryanne knew full well that Lillian had a plan and she never deviated from it. They were seniors now and Lillian was determined to graduate with honors and there were rumblings that she would be valedictorian. After that, Lillian planned to intern at her father's law firm, the first woman to do so. Then perhaps law school. If and when she married, she was certain she did not want a marriage like her parents'. Her parents were grievously unhappy but her father knew that if he ever left, her mother would have nowhere to go, no way to survive. Her mother had only gone to college to find a husband and once she had, she dropped out so she would have ample time to keep a home and be the perfect lawyer's wife. She had no interests outside of the home, no skills that would translate to the real world. That wasn't what Lillian wanted.

Lillian had decided long ago that she wanted a great measure of independence. She wanted to know her own mind, to speak her own mind whenever she pleased and be able to hold her own in a room, especially a room full of men. She pocketed the letter and linked arms with Maryanne. "Let's go. We're late for class."

The letter remained in the pocket of Lillian's blazer until long after dinner that night. She had completely forgotten about it until she was back in her room and went to take off her blazer. It was her habit to always check her pockets before hanging her blazer up because she was notorious for leaving pens, paperclips, and occasionally hard candies in there. The pens would leak, the paperclips rip holes in the lining, and the candies melt. If her mother discovered any of those things there would be hell to pay. Worse if she discovered an uncapped pen when doing laundry, getting ink all over everything. That had happened once and once only when Lillian was in middle school.

The corners of the letter had curled from being in her pocket all day, crushed against her hip as she sat in class. She put it on her desk, then arranged her textbooks next to it, preparing to start work on her assignments. Situating herself at her desk, Lillian wished she had a cup of tea but it would have to wait until she could get downstairs to the kitchen. Right now she had plenty she wanted to see to before her roommate returned from her last class of the day.

Though she had limited time to get things done, she was having a hard time focusing with the letter just sitting there as it was. She looked up at the clock and reasoned that she had a few minutes to satisfy her curiosity. She just couldn't linger. Reaching for her letter opener, she slit open the envelope and slid the composition paper out with her fingertips. It was a piece of cheap paper that likely came from a school boy's composition notebook, folded in four and stuck into any old envelope. Lillian had always imagined correspondence with the right kind of boy would be done on matching stationery embossed with the maker's mark. Maybe her correspondent might even have his own letterhead. But not this boy. This boy made due with whatever was at hand. Lillian wrinkled her nose in disgust.

Unfolding the letter, she found more of the messy, hurried printing. There was no salutation, just her name at top as if from some-one who knew her well, yet her name was misspelled so it wasn't any of her acquaintances. She began to read.

> *Lilianne-*
>
>   *I don't know if you remember me but I'm a friend of Celia Graves, your classmate. I have known her since we were young and I asked her about you. She said such nice things about you that I thought I would write and ask if I might take you out. She liked you very much. Please re-spond as soon as you can.*
>
>   *Joel*

Celia Graves? The first year who had disappeared after Elms Night? Lillian had never been friends with her. In fact, she didn't even know her name until she was reported as missing and Lillian realized she and Betty Farraday were the last two people to see her that night. Whoever Joel was, he was grasping at straws, making a connection that just wasn't there. Lillian folded the letter and tucked it back in the envelope, then stuck it in the back of her desk drawer. He would have to do a little better than that.

CHAPTER THIRTEEN

The next day Nora found herself sitting across from Lillian Hanley's parents, both of whom looked extremely uncomfortable with her presence. They seemed puzzled as to why Nora had turned up because of course she hadn't given much away over the phone, just told them she needed to talk with them about their daughter. Her father, Albert, the now-retired lawyer, wore a stern expression as if he was ready to call out his objections to whatever questions Nora might ask. Lillian's mother, Christine was decked out in a Chanel suit and pearls, tea laid out on their finest china with the most perfect cookies Nora had ever seen. The spread certainly put Betty Farraday's store-bought ones to shame.

It had taken quite a bit of cajoling to get Selena to agree to stay put while Nora went to talk to Lillian's parents. She could tell from Mrs. Hanley's tone when she called that the family wasn't best pleased to be hearing from a writer and they only invited her to their home to avoid being rude. Nora supposed there was also a tinge of curiosity somewhere in there as well. Selena didn't like being left out but Nora tried her best to make her understand that two of them showing up at the Hanleys' door might be a bit more than the family bargained for and might make them less likely to talk.

Now that she was here, Nora was having a hard time deciding where to start. "I just want to say first that I'm very sorry for your loss."

Christine Hanley cleared her throat and wrinkled her nose as if she was smelling something off. "Thank you but I'm sure you're not here to give us your condolences for a girl you never met and who passed before you were even born."

Well, that cut to the quick of it. "No, you're right. That's not the reason I'm here."

"Are you a reporter?" her husband asked, leaning forward and folding his hands, elbows resting on his knees. He was trying to be intimidating but it came off more as an old man playing at being intimidating.

"I'm not. I am a writer, but I write mystery novels." That was clearly not the right answer. Mr. Hanley straightened his back and narrowed his eyes. "I'm not writing about your daughter. I was working on researching something else and just happened on an article about Lillian."

"And you just thought you'd stick your nose in?" His wife's tone was equally cold.

"No Mrs. Hanley. That's not at all what I thought. In fact," Nora leaned forward, her knees brushing the very expensive-looking coffee table that separated her from the Hanleys in their very expensive-looking living room where it was beginning to feel as if the heat wasn't quite working. Or perhaps they weren't as well off as they looked and the heat was off to save money. Either way, Nora had to work to keep from shivering. "In fact, I think Lillian might have had a connection to another young lady who passed the same year."

The Hanleys looked at one another, a look passing between them that Nora couldn't quite decipher. "That Graves girl." It was a statement, not a question. Of course they would know about it. Lillian had likely been questioned extensively once the police realized Lillian was a witness to the kidnapping.

"Yes sir, Celia Graves. It appears Celia was being—" she was hesitant to say "stalked" as that tended to make people unnecessarily uncomfortable. "—followed. She was being followed. By a young man. Likely the young man whose car Lillian saw her get into. I just wondered if Lillian had ever experienced something similar."

Neither of them spoke for quite some time. Mrs. Hanley was looking down at her hands, her fingers twined in her lap. The only thing betraying her inner turmoil and anxiety was the white of her knuckles that had intensified as she wrung her hands tighter. Mr. Hanley gazed off into the middle distance as if he was thinking about something important but Nora could tell he was simply avoiding her question.

Finally, Mrs. Hanley sighed and pried her fingers apart, shaking out her hands that were likely tingling with pins and needles by that point, and twisted her wedding rings back into place. "She received a number of letters. After Celia's disappearance."

Nora was stunned. "Who were they from?"

"That's none of your business," Lillian's father snapped. His wife shot him a look that could have cracked ice.

"They were from a young man. She had no idea who he was but he certainly seemed to know her. After her death, we told the police about the letters but by then they had declared her death to be of natural causes despite the findings in the autopsy."

"You mean the poison?"

Mrs. Hanley's fingers returned to her rings which she spun nervously as she nodded. "It's not an easy thing to talk about, you have to understand. And you have to forgive my husband. He forgets he's not in a courtroom anymore." There was clearly no love lost in this marriage. "The police didn't think the letters meant anything but I kept them anyway. Just in case." She stood up and walked over to a large writing desk that was tucked into the corner of the living room, nestled into a bay window covered with expensive drapes that were so long they pooled on the floor in little eddies of purple silk. Taking a small key out of her pocket, she unlocked one of the pigeon holes and pulled out a packet of letters nearly identical to those that were tucked away in Celia's hidey hole.

"Here. These aren't doing much good locked away in that desk." She handed the letters to Nora then wiped her hands on her skirt as if the letters had left behind something dirty or toxic. "See if you can make something of them. I'll see you out."

Nora could take a hint, especially when it was that far out in the open. "Thank you, Mrs. Hanley." She noticed that Albert hadn't said a word though he was now leaning back into the couch, one leg crossed over the other, trying but failing to look relaxed.

Mrs. Hanley ushered Nora out the door with a smile fixed on her perfectly made up face. "Thank you so much for your visit. No need to return...those," she said, pointing to the letters still clutched in Nora's hand. "Best of luck." With that, she closed the door on Nora still standing on the porch, bewildered by that rather odd visit. She turned on her heel and headed for her car, anxious to get back and go through this second set of letters. In order to get Selena to remain behind Nora had had to agree to bring the letters straight back to the dorm so they could go through them together and, as expected, she was waiting by the door for Nora. "Were you here all night?"

Selena rolled her eyes and held the door open for Nora. "Very funny. Let's go upstairs."

There was a portable kettle boiling away on Selena's desk, two cups set out and ready for tea. Nora handed off the letters to Selena and busied herself making tea for the both of them. Shuffling through the envelopes, Selena put the letters in order as they had with Celia's, from oldest to newest, then opened the first one.

"This must be his first one to Lillian. He's spelled her name wrong." Selena appeared disgusted already by Joel's missive. "Get this, he tells her that Celia is his friend and that she's told him all about Lillian! They didn't even know each other."

"But it's definitely from him?"

Selena nodded and showed Nora the letter. The handwriting matched as did the signature. It was from Joel alright. "I can't believe Lillian's parents had these the whole time."

"They would never have had a reason to think the letters had anything to do with Celia Graves. Like you said, they didn't even know each other." Nora handed her a cup of tea and took the next letter from her.

"From the sound of this one Lillian responded to his first letter just like Celia did. He says again that Celia has said such nice things about Lillian and he's asking her all these first date type questions. What are you studying in school? Where did you grow up?"

"Do you suppose she met up with him?" Selena asked.

Shrugging, Nora opened the next letter. "Well, apparently she did. Listen to this-- 'Dear Lillian'- at least he spelled it correctly this time- 'I so enjoyed having coffee with you. I'm so very glad that Celia mentioned you to me and that I had the nerve to write you. Looking forward to seeing you again."

Selena had skipped to the bottom of the pile and opened the final letter. "Nora, look at this one. I think he was the last person to see her the day she died."

Dear Lillian-

    I enjoyed our lunch today. I'm so very sorry you're not feeling your best but there's no need to apologize. I hope this note gets to you in time. If you see Celia, tell her I said hello.

"Celia had already been found dead by then." Nora raised her eyebrows in surprise. "That's quite a daring move, writing something like that in a letter."

Selena shook the letter at Nora, her face coated in disgust. "I can't believe Lillian's parents didn't put this together!"

"Maybe they didn't read them. Or maybe they didn't pay attention to when they were sent."

"If it was your daughter, wouldn't you be scrutinizing every possible piece of evidence?"

"Not necessarily." Nora took the letter from Selena and examined it under the light from her desk lamp. "Lillian's death had already been put down to natural causes. The autopsy results weren't in for another few days so they wouldn't necessarily have known about the poisoning yet. There was no reason for them to suspect foul play at this point."

The Hanleys had likely just assumed that Lillian had an admirer, someone who had taken her on a date or two and who was diligent in his correspondence. They would have had no reason to question Joel's motives, nor to wonder at what he said about Celia. For all her parents knew, Celia had indeed mentioned Lillian, who was well known on campus, to this boy and suggested he write to her. There were any number of possibilities that a parent, in the throes of grief, would not have thought of.

"Now we have solid proof of a connection between the two girls."

Nodding, Nora began to spin out a possible scenario. "The night that Celia left campus one of the nuns had pulled her aside and said something to her. I wonder if it had something to do with Joel being parked outside. Perhaps the nun told her to get rid of him, thinking it was an innocent thing, and Joel somehow forced Celia into the car. Lillian was too far away to see whether or not she got into the car voluntarily and Betty Farraday only saw Celia from behind. But Lillian was standing directly under the lights at the front of Berchmans when Joel came around the corner so he would have seen her face clearly. He would have known she saw his car but couldn't have known whether or not Celia had ever mentioned him stalking her. So he covers his tracks by finding out who Lillian is and writing to her the very next day as if Celia is still alive in order to cover his tracks."

"That all makes sense," Selena said, lowering herself to the floor with her lukewarm tea in her hand. "But none of that explains the poisoning."

"And how would he have tracked Lillian down? Only her friends would know where to find her and I can't imagine they would have given her information to a stranger. Nor would any of the campus staff." Nora thought for a moment, running the entire thing through again in her head. " Suppose each time he met Lillian it was on campus. Or nearby enough to walk. Suppose she hadn't seen his car until one day, just before her death, she sees his car and realizes that she's seen it before."

"So you think she put it all together and Joel couldn't have that so he poisoned her to keep her quiet?"

"It makes sense." Nora put the letters down and picked up her own cup, cradling it in her hands even though its comforting warmth was long gone. She reached over and turned the kettle back on, intent on refreshing both their cups. "We need to know who the nun was who talked to Celia at Elms Night."

"How are we going to find that out?"

"I know exactly who to ask."

CHAPTER FOURTEEN

They found Sister Eleanor at the pool, where Nora knew she would be, and thankfully the nun was the only one in the water. Nora and Selena stood by the bleachers waiting for Eleanor to come out before ambushing her with questions. She looked at the two of them curiously as she got out and headed for her towel.

"Nora Phillips. Why aren't you in the water? Aren't you supposed to be rehabbing that knee of yours?" She shook out her towel and wrapped it around herself, then shook out her short mop of gray curls.

"I am, but not tonight." Looking quickly at Selena who nodded reassuringly, Nora launched right in. "Remember when I asked you about Lillian the other night?"

Sister Eleanor nodded, crossing her arms across her chest, causing her suit to drip out from under the towel, forming a puddle at her feet. "I do. But I think I told you as much as I know."

"Well, I'm hoping you know one more thing. Do you remember Elms Night that year? 1953?"

"Of course I do. We all do. That was quite a night."

Nodding in understanding, Nora went on. "Do you remember someone, one of the sisters, pulling Celia Graves aside? The freshman who disappeared that year?"

"I thought you wanted to know about Lillian," Eleanor said, her expression stern but unreadable. "Why are you asking about Celia?"

"Did you know Celia was murdered?" Selena interjected.

Sister Eleanor flinched. "Of course I knew."

"There's a lot about that night that's still unclear. I was hoping you remembered who it was that talked to her."

Casting her eyes to the floor, Eleanor dragged her bare big toe through the puddle at her feet and sighed. "It was me."

"What?" Nora thought she couldn't possibly have heard her correctly.

Eleanor met her eye and repeated herself. "I'm the one who talked to her that night."

"And what did you say to her?"

"Ladies," she said hesitantly. "I think this is a conversation that would be best had fully clothed and with a drink in our hands. Give me a few minutes to put myself back together."

Selena raised her eyebrows, spreading her hands palms up as if to say, *What else is there to do?* Nora lifted a shoulder in reply and the two of them waited silently while Sister Eleanor dried off and dressed. When she emerged from the locker room bundled up in her hat and coat, she gestured for the two women to follow her. They left the back door of the Maguire Center and made their way to the very back corner of the campus, tucked behind the chapel where the nuns' residence was hidden amongst a copse of trees. Everyone knew the residence was back there but to the best of Nora's knowledge no student, past or present, had ever stepped foot in it. It was an unspoken rule that it was off limits yet here they were now, trailing after Sister Eleanor who led them up the stairs and to her room which was sparse but surprisingly comfortable, spare but cozy.

There were only two places to sit, the bed and a wooden chair that was wedged under a writing desk, much like the students' dorm rooms. The two women waited while Eleanor bustled around, hanging up her coat, unwinding her scarf from her neck, and pulling the hat from her head. She then rustled around searching for something and came up with three glasses which she promptly filled with brandy from a small bottle that was hidden behind her wardrobe. The small bed was tucked into an alcove, the room shaped like a very short "L" and she settled herself on the edge of the mattress. Nora took the chair, kicking it out so she was facing Sister Eleanor, and Selena chose the floor.

"That night, there was a car idling on Gaylord Street. I happened to be walking back from Gaylord House and the car was just sitting there. I went to the driver's side window and waited for the young man to open it." She took a sip of her brandy and shivered as it went down. "He said he was waiting for Celia Graves, a first year. That she was expecting him. I told him that wasn't possible because Elms Night would be taking her entire evening."

Joel insisted to Sister Eleanor that he and Celia had plans that evening, that he was meant to pick her up. She repeated what she had said about Elms Night, then also reminded him that the girls had a strict curfew. Unless they had written permission from their parents, they were not to leave campus after the dinner hour. He listened, then very gruffly told Sister Eleanor he wasn't leaving without Celia.

"I went back in and found her, pulled her aside, and told her she had two choices. She could go out there and tell her young man to leave, or she could get in his car and forget about coming back to campus." She took another sip of her brandy and shook her head. "If I had only known…"

"Sister, I certainly don't want to make you feel any worse about this," Nora said, "but it appears that after he drove off with Celia, presumably to kill her and dump her body, he set his sights on Lillian."

Eleanor looked up, eyes wide, and Nora could see her hands were shaking. "He what?"

"He wrote to Lillian the day after, telling her that he was a friend of Celia's, that she suggested he get in touch with Lillian."

"We're assuming," Selena broke in, "that he saw Lillian after she closed the doors. He knew she had seen his car. Then he established contact with her and it appears that they met. Frequently."

Dropping her head in her hands, Eleanor let out a sound that was partway between a sigh and a sob. She sounded as if she was choking. "I sent them both to their death is what you're saying."

"No, of course that's not what we're saying at all," Nora objected.

"But in actuality, that's what happened. I poked the bear as they say. I might as well have put Celia in that car myself, then pushed Lillian out in front of it!"

"Actually, you should be grateful he didn't come after you too."

Eleanor stood and went over to her desk, opening the drawer and pulling out a packet of letters. "Oh but he did." The envelopes were addressed to the residence but didn't have a specific name on them. There were no postmarks so it appeared they had been hand-delivered this time. "These seemed to appear in the letter box only on the days that I checked the mail. I opened the first one and knew immediately they were for me."

Unlike the letters to Celia and Lillian, the letters to Eleanor were blatant threats.

"He said I had disrespected him when I spoke to him about Celia. He goes on about how he and Celia were to be married and that I had no authority over her in that matter. Later, he threatens to track me down should I ever mention having talked to him that night or seen his face." Eleanor shook her head, disgusted. "He never signed any of the letters so what would I have reported? What would I have said to anyone? It was days before we knew Celia had been murdered and I had no idea he had moved on to Lillian. I assumed he was long gone."

The three of them sat in silence, Nora worried that Sister

Eleanor might start crying at any moment. "It must have been quite a burden to bear, knowing you had likely spoken to Celia's killer."

"It's something I've carried with me for a very long time. I've prayed over it, confessed to it in my own way, done penance time and again. Now I feel like it wasn't nearly enough."

"You need to know, the police have a journal Celia kept leading up to her disappearance as well as all the letters Joel sent to her." Nora wrung her hands in her lap, her eyes fixed on the glass in Sister Eleanor's hand that shook dangerously. "Lillian's parents gave us the letters Joel wrote to her as well and we'll be passing those on to the police tomorrow morning. You might consider doing the same with those." She gestured at the pile that now lay on the floor in front of Selena. "They may not be signed but the police can certainly match the handwriting. It's rather distinctive."

"I understand. Do with them what you need to. And of course, direct the police my way. I'll tell them everything I know."

Nora nodded, tucking the envelopes in her bag with the others from the Hanleys. "We'll let them know. Thank you for telling us all this Sister. We know it wasn't easy."

Getting up off the floor, Selena murmured her agreement, nodding along with Nora. She had her hands folded contritely in front of her as if she had just stepped out of confession. Nora angled her head towards the door, suggesting it was time for them to leave, letting Selena lead the way. They left Sister Eleanor sitting on her bed looking deflated, as if telling them about Joel had taken the wind out of her sails.

Once they were safely outside Nora heard Selena expel a breath that sounded like she had been holding it the whole time they were in the residence.

"I can't believe she sat on that information for all that time."

"She didn't have the whole picture. There was no way to know it was all connected."

Selena was shaking her head and shivering violently in the cold. Nora realized the girl wasn't wearing a coat. She must have left it in Sister Eleanor's room and now she was freezing.

"Come on. Let's get back inside. I need to make a phone call."

Grabbing Selena's hand, Nora practically dragged her back to O'Leary Hall, then yanked the lanyard out of Selena's pocket to key open the door. They blew past the RA who yelled after them to sign in but they didn't stop. They pounded up the stairs and didn't stop moving until they got to the alcove outside of Selena's room where Nora pushed her onto the steam radiator to warm up. When she finally stopped shivering Nora unlocked her room and Selena went in, falling immediately onto her bed and rolling herself up in the comforter. Nora pulled out her phone and dialed Dave's number.

She growled in frustration when she got his voicemail. "Call me. As soon as you get this. It's important." Hanging up, she turned the volume up on her phone so she would hear it when Dave called back, then jammed it back in her pocket. The moment she did, she heard her email ding and she pulled her phone back out to find a message from Eric in her inbox.

To: Nora.Phillips1028@gmail.com
From: eric.silva@greenmountainediting.com

Subject: It better be good…

That was it. Nothing in the body of the email. Nora slapped the heel of her hand against her forehead. That was Eric's passive-aggressive way of letting her know that his patience was running out. Nora may have made him a pile of money over the years but now he was worrying there might be an end to the gravy train. That his star writer

143

might finally have run out of steam.

Nora wished she could explain to him what it was like to be put in a box that was labeled "Mystery Writer" and taped shut with multiple layers of tape. She loved mysteries. Mysteries had been her life blood since she was little when she used to hide under her bed reading Sherlock Holmes stories. Of course those were mixed in with her Christopher Pike novels and R.L. Stine paperbacks but what did it matter if she loved the classics or devoured the pulp? While other kids were watching cartoons, Nora was watching *Masterpiece Theater* on PBS. She was just one of those people with mystery in her blood.

Now, all these years later, Nora wanted a break. She wanted to at least *try* something different but Eric had stamped that out of her without a second thought. He had no idea what that new manuscript had meant to her, what that shift in her work had meant to her. Eric was watching the gravy train while Nora was searching for the light at the end of the tunnel. She didn't feel like a writer anymore; she was a factory. A plot factory, churning out bestsellers that all had the same general story arc, the same characters, the same setting, the same damned town square. It was all too much.

"Nora? Is everything ok?"

She turned and stuck her head in the room to find Selena burrowed into the covers still shivering. "Yeah everything is ok. Dave, my cop friend, didn't pick up but I left him a message. Hopefully he'll call me back pretty soon."

"Ok," Selena sighed, snuggling down farther and closing her eyes. Nora hoped she wasn't about to die of hypothermia but she needed to get home. She was freezing, exhausted, and suddenly starving despite having eaten that mediocre chicken with Jacqueline earlier.

"I'm going to head home. I'll let you know when I talk to Dave." The only response was a light snore that issued from under the covers. Selena had fallen asleep. Nora turned off her desk lamp and tiptoed out of the room, quietly easing the door shut behind her.

Nora drove home slowly, all the while replaying the conversation with Sister Eleanor. She felt terrible for the nun who thought that she was just doing her job by chasing away a male suitor and laying down the law with one of the students. It was what any one of the nuns would have done in that situation, never supposing it would have such dire consequences for not one but two young women. Now she would have to tell the entire story all over again to the police who, Nora knew, would sit in judgment, asking her why she didn't think to come forward with any of this information before now. It was going to be difficult for her and quite the scandal for the school. The publicity alone. Nora didn't even want to think about it.

Her phone rang as she was pulling into her driveway. She put the car in park and picked up the call. "Hi Dave."

"Something tells me I'm not going to like this."

"No, probably not. You know that journal I had you hand over to your detective friends?"

Nora thought she heard him banging his head on something. Probably his keyboard. "Yea. What about it?"

"There's more."

"More what?"

"More information. Mostly letters from that Joel guy. He was definitely stalking Celia. Then he turned his sights on another girl."

"Oh for....alright. I'll be over after my shift. And Nora?"

"Yeah?"

"Please don't find anything else while you're waiting."

CHAPTER FIFTEEN

By the time Dave showed up Nora was having a hard time keeping her eyes open but she stayed awake long enough to tell Dave everything she had learned. "I've been trying to write it all down as I go so I made a copy of my notes and put it with the letters."

She handed him the pile of envelopes that she had labeled so he would know who the recipient was. "The ones that were sent to Sister Eleanor aren't signed but I figure someone can make the professional call on the handwriting similarities."

"Do you have any idea what kind of a mess this is going to make?" Pressing his palms into his eyes for a moment, Dave stifled a yawn and took the envelopes from her. "I'll make sure the detectives get this. But this time they're definitely going to want to talk to you. And probably these other two women too. Hope you're all ready for that."

"We are. I promise."

"You better be. Because it's my neck on the line, vouching for a writer. You know cops hate writers."

Laughing Nora replied, "I thought they hated journalists."

Dave waved off her comment as he headed out the door. "Same thing."

Once he was gone Nora turned off the exterior lights and checked to make sure the door was locked though she wasn't sure what she was so afraid of. Even if they did track down Joel after all these years he was no longer a young man. It was highly unlikely he was still lurking around out there but there were times when Nora couldn't control the chill that traveled up her spine, the urge to get away from the darkened windows and turn off all the lights, the need to check under the bed for monsters.

"The long and short is, we're pretty sure Joel Sanders isn't even his real name." It had been three days and Dave's detective friend, Sam Calvanese had gone through every page of Celia's journal and every letter Nora and Selena had managed to assemble. He had interviewed both them and Sister Eleanor, and was planning to speak with Betty Farraday and Alice Graves Montgomery. Lillian's parents remembered her going to a party with a young man by the name of Sanders but other than that they had no leads, nothing to go on, and no way to figure out who Joel really was.

"Ok thanks for keeping me posted Dave." Nora hung up with a sigh and shook her head to let Selena know they hadn't come up with anything. "Now what?"

"Now we do the one thing you haven't gotten to yet," she said, curled up on on the throw pillows piled on the floor of Nora's office where they had set up shop for the foreseeable future, a cup of tea in her hand.

Nora was puzzled. "What's that?"

"Track down the families who lived on Gaylord Street back in the day."

That was going to be a hell of a lot of work but Selena was right, it was the one base they hadn't yet covered. But Nora had another idea.

"Aren't we close to the anniversary of them finding Celia's body?"

Selena glanced at the calendar hanging on the wall above Nora's desk. "You're right. I didn't even think about that."

"We need to find out where Celia is buried." Nora said, pulling out her phone. "And I know just who to ask." She dialed Alice's number and waited, hoping her son wouldn't pick up, but luck was not on Nora's side.

"Hello?"

"Hi. Can I speak to Alice please?"

Silence greeted her from the other end of the line. "No. You can't."

"Excuse me?"

"My mother should have listened to me the first time you came around here, digging into my great aunt's disappearance. Now the police are crawling all over us and my mother has had to relive that entire thing…" There was a scuffle and it sounded like the receiver had been dropped, then Alice's voice cut through the static.

"Hello, Nora? Are you still there?"

"Yes I'm still here." She could hear Alice covering the mouthpiece and hissing at Steven, yelling at him for trying to get Nora off the phone. "I'll talk to her if I want to Steven. I'm a grown woman for heaven's sake! I'm so sorry for my son's behavior Nora. He's been a little...prickly lately. He acts like he was there, like he's the one reliving everything. It's not your story Steven! You never even met her. You stop being rude to everyone. I mean it. He's been so much worse since his father passed."

"I'm so sorry to hear that Alice. I didn't realize you'd lost your husband too."

Alice sighed. "It's quite alright. That's what happens when you get to be my age. More dead than alive, family and friends alike."

"Listen Alice, I called to ask you a very specific question about Celia."

"Yes, go ahead Nora."

"I need to know where Celia is buried."

"Well sure," Alice replied. "She's in St. Thomas right up the street here."

Why hadn't Nora thought of that? That was the most logical place for her to be buried. Now that she thought about it, she remembered seeing a St. Thomas School sticker in the rear window of the one and only vehicle parked in Alice's driveway.

"Thank you so much Alice. I have a theory that I want to test. I'll keep you posted!"

"No problem Nora. Thank you so much for everything. I know Steven. Pipe down!" The phone clattered against the cradle and the line went dead. Nora laughed, imagining the dressing down Alice was giving her son right that moment. "Ok. I know where she's buried now. We're still a few days from the anniversary so in the meantime, let's do some homework on those houses."

Nora pulled up a current map of the street and printed it out. "We'll have to go down to the town hall. We'll need to match these houses with the houses that were there in 1953, then figure out who the owners were. Hopefully there's at least one original family still there."

"Then let's go. I need to be doing something to keep busy."

Thankfully the town hall wasn't busy and they were able to get right in and talk to a clerk who found the street listings for them fairly quickly. Not much had changed with the exception of houses that had been demolished to make way for the freshman dorm and the college center; they didn't want to discount those houses just because they weren't there anymore. Nora jotted down house numbers while Selena asked the clerk for street listings from that year.

"Here you go ladies. This is the neighborhood directory for 1953." The clerk was a sturdy looking older woman with her graying hair tied back in a neat chignon and a pair of reading glasses perched on the bridge of her nose. "Some of those houses aren't there anymore you know."

Nora nodded, only vaguely listening to the clerk.

"My house was one of the ones demolished when they built Rose William. I was so sad to see that house go."

"You lived on Gaylord?" Nora snapped to attention, her pencil hovering over the list of addresses she had jotted in her notebook. "Were you there in 1953?"

The clerk smiled. "The fact that you can't be reasonably sure I'm that old makes me very happy. Yes I was there in 1953. I was seven years old. What is it you're looking for?"

"I'm trying to track down a car that was parked there on the night of September 13th."

The clerk pulled out a chair and sat across from Nora, slipping her glasses off and rubbing her eyes. "You're looking into the Celia Graves disappearance."

"I am, yes. Do you remember anything from back then?"

"You know, it's funny," she said in a tone that said it wasn't really funny at all. "When something terrible happens, the police say they'll investigate any possible lead no matter how small. What they don't say is that they don't want leads from someone small."

"You tried to talk to the police?" Selena asked, incredulous. "What did they say?"

"I told them I'd seen a car that night. And a number of other nights too. Sometimes it was parked there running, with a boy inside. Other times it was just the car. I could see it from my bedroom window but the police wouldn't listen. They just said I had an active imagination for a little girl." She put active imagination in air quotes. "I tried to tell them I had seen the license plate but they didn't want to hear it."

"You had a license plate and they ignored you?" Nora couldn't believe that the police had been so short sighted but the clerk was right, it happened all the time. "I'm sorry, I didn't even introduce myself before I started grilling you. I'm Nora Phillips and this is Selena Petersen."

"Pleasure to meet you both. I'm a big fan of your books Miss Phillips. And I'm Judy Windham. Though I was a Miller back then." "It's nice to meet you Judy. I don't suppose you still remember that license plate number do you?"

Judy nodded. "Of course I do. I wrote it down just in case someone ever came to talk to me again. Excuse me for just one second." She went behind the counter and grabbed her bag, pulling out a leather bound notebook that looked a lot like Celia's. "I write everything down. Thoughts, ideas, things I don't want to forget." She unwound the leather tie and opened to the front cover of the book where, under her name and address was the license plate from Joel's car. "I wrote it in the front of my journal back then and I've copied it over to every notebook I've had since then."

She pushed the notebook over to Nora who added the plate number to her copy of the timeline. She had kept the original but made a photocopy for the police, though she wasn't sure if they had even wanted or needed it. "This is extremely helpful Judy. You've saved us a lot of leg work."

"If only the police had felt the same way back then!" Judy closed her notebook and patted it lovingly. "I hope you can do something with it."

"Me too. We'll let you know what happens." Nora gathered her things and she and Selena headed back out into the day. "It's too bad."

"What is?" Selena asked, sliding into the passenger seat of Nora's car.

"The license plate. It's probably not going to do us much good."

"Why not?"

Nora started the car and headed for home. "It's from 1953. The odds that the registry maintains those records are slim."

"So we're still exactly where we were this morning."

"Essentially. But at least someone saw the car besides Betty and Lillian."

"I guess," Selena sighed. "But that doesn't tell us anything more about this guy. Is he still alive? Is he still around?"

"If my theory is right, we'll find out when Celia's anniversary rolls around."

"You think he'll come back to the grave?"

"I have a feeling, yes. He was so deeply enamored of her. He was in love with her."

Selena had thought the same but then he had moved on to Lillian so soon after Celia's death. "What if he was just a garden variety stalker who didn't care who he followed?"

"I don't think he was that. When you read those letters, the tone is very different." Nora thought back to the two piles of letters. "I think he just wanted to be friends with Lillian."

"And they were such good friends that he turned around and poisoned her just for fun?"

Nora had wondered about that too. They were both assuming that Joel was responsible for Lillian's death too but so far neither of them could think of a reason why he would have killed Lillian. "I don't know why he poisoned Lillian. If he was even the one who did it. He might not have been. For all we know Lillian was poisoned accidentally."

"But it makes more sense if Joel poisoned her."

"I'm leaning that way of course, but we need a lot more information."

Nora pulled out her phone and called Dave, leaving the license plate number on his voicemail. There was no chance she or Selena could dig into the registry, it would have to be done by law enforcement and it would likely take some time so all they could do now was wait. While Selena was on campus finishing up the fall semester, Nora sat at her desk and pieced together everything she had written, slowly editing the story and shaping it into something readable. What had started out as fragmented case notes, was slowly molded into something new and fresh– a Charley Donahue mystery with a twist, a special guest star that was proving worth her weight in gold by livening up Nora's typical cozy plot line. The change of setting was refreshing too, pulling Charley out of her comfort zone and away from the little town that had made Nora's novels feel so stiflingly familiar.

She wrote for days, tucked up in her office with Hank and Lulu wandering in and out, the quiet of the house insulating her against the cold outside. Every so often Selena would call and check in but so far there had been no news from the police, nothing to share but it didn't take long for word to get out that there was an investigation happening and that somehow a New York Times bestselling mystery author was involved.

"Nora, it's Eric. Why am I getting calls from news outlets asking for comment on your investigation? What the hell are they talking about?"

The other line beeped as she tried to explain to Eric everything that had happened. Dave was trying to call just as a slew of text messages poured in. "Eric, I have to let you go. I have another call coming in that I have to take."

"Nora…" Eric was cut off as Nora picked up Dave's call.

"Someone leaked to the press. There's a front page write up on MassLive." Dave sounded absolutely furious. "They couldn't keep their mouths shut for just a few more days." The only thing that was keeping Dave from losing it completely was the knowledge that Nora, Selena, and Sister Eleanor had all already given their statements so at least that part of the investigation would be safe. "But if this Joel guy is still alive, we just tipped our hand."

"And handed him Nora Phillips on a silver platter."

Dave sighed. "I know. Please keep your doors locked until we figure out what to do here."

Chapter Sixteen

Nora went back and forth, trying to decide whether or not she should warn Selena but she reasoned that she would see the news report and that would be warning enough. The media hadn't picked up on Selena's name yet but she and Nora had been seen around campus together enough that her name would come up eventually. Her doors were locked, her curtains drawn, but she couldn't help the fear that was creeping in little by little. She went through and methodically checked everything a second time before gathering up her laptop and heading upstairs with Lulu and Hank, certain she wouldn't get a wink of sleep but knowing she would feel much more comfortable tucked up on the second floor where no one could see in but she could look down on the front of the house where the shadows lengthened across the snow.

With her cell phone at her side and her ears tuned for any sound that might be out of the ordinary, Nora tucked herself into bed and revisited everything she and Selena had collected so far. Dave had said they were fairly certain that Joel Sanders was an alias and where Nora had felt some satisfaction in putting the pieces together, it now felt as if they had assembled a case against a ghost. This man who was almost certainly responsible for the deaths of at least two girls was nothing more than an amorphous threat, just another face in the crowd going about his life as if nothing had happened.

Of course there were plenty of cold cases that had been solved decades later like the kidnapping and murder of the counter girl at the book shop in Nora's hometown whose killer was caught nearly thirty years later but that case was solved because someone had had the foresight to collect physical evidence from the crime scene that was preserved until DNA science was sophisticated enough to find a match. There was no physical evidence that could potentially unmask Joel Sanders because it was 1953 and the police would never have dreamed that one day a hair or a fiber could lead them to a killer. Instead the dump site where Celia's body was found was now a vacant lot next to an abandoned building that was slated for demolition and Lillian, well no one had even considered Lillian's death to be anything other than natural so there was never a second thought.

Sighing, Nora closed her laptop and leaned back while she buried her fingers in Hank's silky fur. His rumbling purrs vibrated through her fingertips as he snoozed, not a care in the world. "Oh to be a cat, right Hank?" He opened one eye, a slit of gold and gave a flick of his tail as if in agreement then went back to sleep. "Not a care in the world." Nora picked up a paperback novel and tried to get lost in the pages but she was on such high alert that she couldn't get into it. Instead, she eyed the bottle of muscle relaxers her surgeon had also prescribed and imagined drifting off into a mindless, painless sleep. "Well it certainly couldn't hurt..."

The temperature had dropped substantially as night fell and the air had gathered up the incoming frost. Nora turned up the thermostat and headed to bed with just enough energy to get out of her clothes before crawling under the blankets. As the pain pill kicked in, Nora felt herself slipping into a soft, warm level of unconsciousness that rendered her stress free and miraculously ready for rest. It occurred to her as she drifted off that she would be left defenseless if someone broke into the house but she wasn't awake long enough to dwell. She slept heavily, exhaustion finally catching up with her but it wasn't long before she found herself back on the Elms campus, walking the halls of O'Leary in a blue taffeta dress and low heels, a flower corsage on her wrist as the faint strains of music followed her past rows of closed doors, rooms that sat silently behind metal numbers that had been tacked to them. Nora knew she was on the first floor though she realized that, even in her waking life, she had never walked past these rooms. In all the years she had lived in that building, all the time she spent thinking about O'Leary Hall and imagining its walls, she had never seen any of the rooms on the first floor. It had only ever been a pass-by as she ran upstairs or headed out to class.

The hallway had a gauzy feel, the lighting muted by sconces that were yellowed by age. It was how Nora remembered the light in there, especially on days when it rained and O'Leary opened its arms to the girls, drawing them into the warmth and coziness that only an old building can offer. O'Leary was seasonal. Nora arrived each year as the last breath of summer eased into the golden swirl of fall, leaves already turning on the trees that dotted the campus. The dorm remained her home through the first rainfall of October and the frosts of December right up to the edge of Christmas break. Once Nora and Margaret returned in January, they were deep into a New England winter that would carry them through the white heavy snow that turned into the gray, dirty ice of February and March when the cycle would complete itself, rolling into the frigid April rain that signaled the nearing of the end of the school year.

O'Leary was never summer, much like Nora's favorite mystery shows. The sunlight was never full and warm, there was never a yearning for the beach or other summer activities. Instead, Nora and Margaret ate their ice cream in the dead of winter as their feet froze in boots that never fully stayed dry. In fact even now, in her dreams, Nora felt the tendrils of cold air that fluttered along the worn green carpeting and traveled up and down the stairs like a solid entity that she could reach out and touch. She swayed in the direction of the piano room but that was not the source of the music. Instead the notes floated up to her from the basement, tripping up the stairs and surrounding her, nudging her towards the stairs and leading her down them.

In the basement, the doors to the study that she and Margaret had loved so much were propped open and the sound of voices spilled out into the hallway where Nora stood, watching the light bend across the basement walls, lighting up dresses and bowties, shiny shoes and shiny hair. She breathed in, then slowly out, whispering, *"The party."*

1953

Lillian waited on the steps of O'Leary Hall for Joel to pick her up. They were going to walk down and get a slice of pizza. She enjoyed spending time with Joel, though she was beginning to think he was more invested in their friendship than she was as his letters were bordering on romantic. Lillian had tried to temper that by making her letters as chummy as she could, reminding him that she would be working after graduation and wasn't going to have time for friends. Emphasis on friends. In fact, this was going to be the last time she went out with him. She didn't want to give him the wrong idea and she wanted to let him down easy so this was it, the last time she would accept one of his invites, the last time she would meet him on the steps.

"Hi Joel!" Lillian came down the steps to meet him, greeting him with a quick half hug. "So, pizza?"

"Absolutely!" Sometimes Joel worried that Lillian might be getting the wrong idea about him. He was beginning to think perhaps he was coming on too strong, making her think he was interested in all the wrong ways. But then, maybe she needed to think he was interested in order for her to ask him to the senior party, a topic he planned to

bring up on their walk. "Say, I was wondering. I heard there was a party coming up and, well, I've never been to a college party before…"

Joel let his voice trail off, giving the impression that he was
just a shy, friendly guy who wanted a chance to see what all the fuss
was about but Lillian's face fell immediately.

"Listen Joel. I've been meaning to talk to you about something…" She too trailed off, but he could tell it wasn't a calculated
move. She was genuinely trying to figure out what to say to him.
"You're a really great guy…"

"Oh no!" He stopped her right there in the middle of the sidewalk and decided to try to mediate the situation before she could cut
him off completely. "I'm so sorry Lillian. I hope I didn't give you the
wrong idea. I like you a lot, but just as a good pal." He hung his head
and stuck his hands in his pocket, doing his best to look like a guy who
had given a girl the wrong end of the stick. "I hope you didn't think
otherwise."

Lillian looked surprised, so surprised that she couldn't seem to
get her mouth to work. "Joel, I'm so sorry. I thought…well it doesn't
matter what I thought now does it. You're right, we're pals. It's just
when you mentioned the party—"

"—you thought I was asking you on a date?" Joel replied
sheepishly. "Aw, no. I just wanted to go so I could see what it was like.
I didn't go to college and I've always wondered."

"Then if that's the case, why not? I think it'll be fun!" Lillian
turned and started walking again, her nut brown ponytail bouncing
from side to side as she half-walked, half-skipped in her saddle shoes,
her skirt swishing in time with her hair.

Joel exhaled quietly, relieved that he had managed to keep
the entire thing from derailing. The party itself didn't matter. All he
needed was ample time to slip upstairs in O'Leary Hall while all its
residents were occupied.

CHAPTER SEVENTEEN

Nora sprang out of bed and up the stairs to her office where she fired up her laptop. The house was dark and quiet, the animals still fast asleep in Nora's bed, completely unaware that she had vacated their cozy nest of blankets for the nighttime chill that had settled over the other rooms. As soon as her desktop appeared she opened the folder where she had stashed the party images from the yearbook, then pulled Lillian's obituary from Ancestry to compare. With the images blown up so that she could see faces, Nora combed each and every one until she found her in a mint green taffeta dress with a full skirt and tiny rosettes sewn onto the bodice. She was standing against the wall with a glass of punch in her hand, her mouth open wide in the middle of telling a story, her other hand blurred with motion as she made her point. Zooming out just enough to see the whole group at once, Nora then focused on the male faces, unsure what she was looking for but she would know it when she saw it– a look, an expression, something that would tell her which one of these boys did not belong.

And suddenly there he was, standing off to the side just behind Lillian, looking uncomfortable in an ill-fitting suit and drab tie that looked like a discarded Father's Day gift. He had dark hair, almost black, that fell across his forehead in a silky wave almost hiding his eyes which were also almost black, though that might have been a trick of the light. His skin was fair, pockmarked with acne scars, his cheeks flushed red. The word that came to mind when Nora studied him was furtive, like he was planning something but of course, she could have been imagining it, her brain working overtime from excitement and lack of sleep.

"Are you Joel?" Nora whispered to the photo, running her index finger over the pixelated features of his face. And if this was Joel, what was he doing there with Lillian? Nora had a hard time imagining Lillian inviting someone like him to be her date, not after those letters. By all accounts, Lillian was exceptionally intelligent, talented, and driven. Why would she be spending time with someone like Joel whose poorly written letters were barely legible?

Perhaps she was just being nice. And what had being nice gotten her? Poisoned, that's what it had gotten her. Nora composed an email to Dave and attached the photo, apologizing to him for finding something else when he had begged her not to. Luckily Dave knew her well enough to know that she wasn't going to stop digging until she had all the answers. As she hit send, she looked up and realized that the sun had begun to peek through the curtains and another morning had snuck up on her. She could hear Hank downstairs prowling around the kitchen, already looking for mischief. Her bed called out to her but she knew if she went back to bed she would sleep the day away and that was the last thing she wanted to do.

Grabbing her robe from the foot of her bed, Nora marveled at Lulu's ability to sleep through just about anything. The dog was wrapped up in blankets, the tip of her snout and two front paws the only things sticking out from the cocoon. *If only humans could sleep like that*, Nora thought, pulling her robe tight around her waist and heading for the kitchen to make herself a cup of tea.

As she watched the kettle come to a boil, Nora thought she heard a sound outside. Hank must have heard it too; he jumped onto the counter and pressed his nose to the window above the sink, the one that looked out over the front yard. His ears perked and his whiskers twitched– there was something out there. For a moment, Nora stood and looked out over Hank's shoulder, wondering if it was just a squirrel or even one of the neighbors' cats. But then it clicked, the noise she had heard, it was the mailbox closing.

Without thinking or heeding Dave's warning to stay inside, Nora opened the front door and crossed the lawn to the bank of mailboxes at the edge of the road. She reached out for the tongue on the mailbox door, then stopped herself, remembering what Sister Eleanor had said about Joel hand-delivering his missives to her, his threats. Nora pulled her sleeve over her hand, then pulled open the box where she found yesterday's mail piled haphazardly inside but that wasn't what caught her eye. On the top of the pile, neatly placed on top of the bills and fan letters, was a plain envelope with her name written on it in pencil. With her fingers still protected by the sleeve of her robe, Nora pulled the envelope out of the mailbox and turned it over, carefully sliding the letter out of the unsealed envelope. There was no mistaking the handwriting, the note had come from Joel.

> *Dear Nora-*
> *I saw the news. I know you've been asking questions about me and about Celia and Lillian. I don't appreciate you digging all this up. They were my friends and I miss them very much.*
> *Joel*

Nora rushed inside, locking the door behind her and throwing the deadbolt. Joel not only knew who she was from the news report, he knew where to find her.

She had always been exceptionally careful with her personal life. Once the Charlie Donahue books took off and she decided to purchase her own house she formed a corporation that became her entire business enterprise with no public connection to her or to Charlie Donahue. Her house was owned by that corporation and all of her mail went either to a P.O. Box or to her agent which means Joel had either done some serious digging to find her…

"Or he's been following me." She flipped the letter out of her hand and let it flutter onto the coffee table like something rotten or poisonous, throwing the envelope on top of it. Somewhere upstairs she could hear her cell phone ringing and Lulu grumbling as the noise continued. The ringer stopped just as Nora got to the bedroom, the phone teetering on the edge of her nightstand. She had missed four calls from Selena.

"Finally!" Selena answered on the first ring; she had probably had the phone in her hand waiting for Nora to call.

"I was outside, I didn't hear my phone. What's wrong?"

"He found me. He found me and he slid a letter under my door Nora."

Joel. He had been following them both. "Did you touch it?"

"No. I saw the handwriting on the outside of the envelope and knew it was from him."

"Good," Nora sighed. "Leave it where it is. I'm calling Dave."

"Nora, wait…"

"What Selena?"

A small sigh escaped, amplified by the tinny speaker on her cell phone. "Did you get one too?"

"Yes. I got one too. He found us both."

Dave was, understandably, exasperated when Nora called him, especially as it was barely 7:00 am when he picked up the phone. "This better be good."

"It's not," Nora replied, looking down at the note on the counter as if it might burst into flame at any moment. "I sent you an email earlier. I think I found a photograph of the letter writer but it's from 1953."

"Should be super helpful. There's no way you woke me up on my day off for that."

"No, no I did not. It looks like you were right about the news report. It riled him up."

Dave sighed heavily and Nora could hear him sitting up in bed. "And how do you know that?"

"Because Selena and I both just got hand-delivered notes from him."

He swore vigorously and Nora could hear his wife in the background asking him who it was. Dave shushed her and said something about the biggest pain ever. There was a bit of a commotion as Dave got all the way out of bed and thundered down the stairs into his own kitchen. "Explain yourself Phillips."

"I woke up early this morning after having a dream about Lillian and Joel. Something clicked and I got up to look at some yearbook photos I had found. They were candids from a senior party in 1963 and I found Joel in one of the photos."

"That's great. Get to the part where the psychopath figured out where you live and left you a love note."

"I was making tea and I heard the mailbox go. When I went out there–"

"You went out there by yourself? After I warned you to stay inside and be careful?"

Nora sighed and pinched the bridge of her nose, feeling a headache coming on. "Yes, I went out there by myself and yes, I know it was a stupid thing to do but I wasn't thinking. However, I was thinking enough to cover my hand before I touched the mailbox and the letter itself."

"That's something at least." Dave was running the water in his kitchen, probably making coffee now that Nora had interrupted his one chance to sleep in. "I'll send someone by to pick up those letters so neither of you have to leave."

Peering out her front window, Nora shook her head. "Looks like your officer will only have to make one stop. Selena just pulled into my driveway."

"Oh for…they're already on the way."

Selena knocked on the front door as Nora hung up with Dave. Barreling through the open door and into Nora's living room, Selena paced in front of the couch while chewing on her thumbnail.

"Relax Selena. You're going to wear a hole in my rug." Selena stopped pacing momentarily and stared at Nora. "How are you so calm right now?"

"The police are on their way. Do you have your letter?"

She pulled a Ziploc bag out of her pocket and threw it on top of Nora's letter, still lying on the coffee table. "How do you think he found us?"

"You haven't seen the news?" Selena shook her head. "Some-one leaked Joel's name. There was a story and it mentions me. But my guess is he's been following us," Nora replied honestly, hoping the idea of Joel stalking them wouldn't panic Selena. "But if you really think about it, this is a good thing."

That certainly got a reaction from Selena. "A good thing? Are you kidding me, Nora? We have a murderer following us."

Nora shook her head. "No, we have a presumed murderer fol-lowing us. And the fact that he felt compelled to reach out to both of us and threaten us means we're actually on to something."

"I'm so glad you can find a silver lining in all this but I'm freaking out."

This was one of those times when "I told you so" was beyond inappropriate but Nora couldn't help thinking that Selena had set this whole thing in motion, convincing Nora that there was something to investigate, that there was something not quite right with Lillian and Celia's deaths. But then, Nora was the adult here, the one who could have said no and walked away and yet, here they both were.

"I should have listened to Sister Eleanor," Nora muttered.

"What was that?" Selena asked, leaning in like the detective in an Agatha Christie film, cupping her hand behind her ear.

"Sister Eleanor warned me about digging into this story. She told me it would only make trouble and I should have listened to her."

Just then, there was a strong knock on the door, likely the officer Dave had sent coming to pick up the letters. Nora headed for the door and reached for the knob just as it burst open on its own, swinging hard on its hinges as Nora thought, *maybe a vintage front door wasn't the best idea after all.*

1953

Celia was proud of herself for finding that hiding spot under the sill. It was the perfect place to hide all of his letters where no one else would find them unless they found her journal. And if they found her journal that meant something had happened to her and in that case, she no longer cared who read her innermost thoughts.

Joel's letters had become increasingly unsettling. He talked about Celia as if he had some sort of claim on her that he most certainly did not. She had tried to tell her parents about it but they were too busy with their granddaughter, Alice, to listen. Her brother James was the apple of their eye while Celia was an afterthought, an unwelcome surprise. By the time she came along her parents were already thinking about retirement, about traveling and spending holidays at their grown son's house rather than changing diapers and putting on a show for birthdays and Christmas because they had a small child to raise.

Instead, since she had no one to confide in, Celia had kept copious notes in her journal every time she had seen Joel drive by the house, every time he called and hung up because her father had answered. Little did Joel know that Celia was not allowed to answer the telephone so he would never hear her voice. She also noted everything she knew about him including his license plate number, what color his hair was, and what he wore each time she caught a glimpse of him.

Now that she was away at college she had hoped he wouldn't be able to find her but somehow he had found out where she was. He had probably gotten hold of a yearbook. The high school had listed everyone's college choice plain as day. Celia's heart sank the day he drove by her and called her name while she kept walking, pretending not to know him. Her roommate must have thought she was awful rude but she didn't care. She wasn't about to encourage someone like Joel.

Instead she would watch him just as closely as he had watched her. She would be sure that, should anything happen, the police would know right where to go. In fact, the next time she saw him drive by she thought she might follow him like he did her, see if she could figure out where he lived. Wouldn't that be something if she could lead the police right to him. But she never got the chance.

Elms Night was supposed to be a new beginning, a chance to see what her future might hold, but instead it devolved into a nightmare. The first thing she saw when she walked into Berchmans was the nun's face, clouded over and twisted with anger. She grabbed Celia's elbow and pulled her aside, her fingertips cutting into the soft flesh of her arm.

"There is a young man outside who had some choice words, let me tell you. I told him to move it along and I won't tell you what he said. Suffice it to say that it was impolite." The nun shook herself as if ridding herself of his words. "Now, I suggest you do one of two things. Either you go out there and tell that young man to get lost, or you get in his car and leave, never to come back. Do you hear me?"

Celia was at a loss for words, struck by the vehemence of the nun's words, spat at her much like her mother would have. Pulling away from the nun's grasp, Celia turned and ran outside. It was time to confront Joel. Her journal was tucked safely under the floorboards in her room with everything inside that anyone could ever need to find him.

CHAPTER EIGHTEEN

Joel was taller than Nora expected. Despite his age and mop of gray hair, he was surprisingly fit and shockingly quick. He slammed the door behind him and pressed forward, catching Nora off guard. She stumbled, feeling her knee pop sickeningly as it went one way and her foot another. The hardwood floor came at her fast, her hands stretched back to try to break her fall but her entire body weight was pulling her down, her legs useless.

"Nora!" Selena lurched forward and reached for Nora but Joel was faster, reaching out and grabbing Selena's arm and pulling her to him in a bear hug.

He held her tight as Nora scrambled backward until she felt the newel post dig into her spine. "What do you want?"

"I told you I wanted to meet." His voice was deep, raspy like a smoker's voice. Nora studied his face, certain now that he was definitely the boy in the photo from the party. The close set eyes and long, thin nose were the same. "But then I saw this one–" he jerked Selena like a ragdoll. "I saw this one pull up and storm into your house and I figured, why not talk to the two of you together."

"So you bust open my door like a common criminal and think we're going to what, sit here and have tea?" Nora's knee was already throbbing and she could feel the leg of her pants getting tighter as it swelled. Pain often cut down on her verbal filters.

Joel actually laughed. "I heard you were feisty but..." He chuckled and shook his head as if he couldn't believe Nora would have the nerve to talk back to him. "You know, Celia was feisty. She fought back. That turned out to be a mistake."

That was when Nora saw it, that look in his eyes that turned them nearly black, that told the casual observer there was something missing here. In Joel's case, it was a conscience. He talked about Celia without remorse, without feeling. "And what about Lillian?"

"Lillian didn't have a chance to fight," Joel hissed. "I learned my lesson the first time."

1953

Joel needed Lillian to trust him enough to invite him on campus in the evening when he could sneak into the dorms undetected. He knew there was a senior class party coming up where the girls were allowed to invite whomever they chose and he was hoping he had positioned himself well enough that Lillian would bring him along.

He had already learned from her that the college had not moved anyone into Celia's room after her body was found, and just before she died Celia had told him that she kept a journal and it was hidden somewhere in the dorm. She had yelled it at him, practically spat it at him, while he sat in his car after getting snapped at by that nun. Celia said she had written down everything so that if anything ever happened to her, someone would know where to find him. At the time Joel had absolutely no intention of hurting her. Quite the opposite in fact. He wanted to marry her, give her a home, love her. He had fallen in love with her the first time he saw her at the counter at Forbes and Wallace. She was beautiful with her long red hair and her flashing blue eyes. She was perfect.

Following women was something Joel had gotten really good at. He practiced blending in on the busy city streets of Springfield, ducking in and out of store fronts, turning at the exact moment one of them stopped to see if someone was behind them. Celia was no different. He watched her shop at Johnson's Books, peered in the windows of Red Rose while she had lunch with her family. A family he could tell wasn't very kind to her, judging by the way they smiled and fawned over her brother and the brother's wife but barely acknowledged Celia's existence. That was alright though. Joel would make up for that by making sure she knew she was the only person Joel cared about.

Occasionally he would loiter in the parking lot at her high school, pretending to be there picking up a sibling. He would follow her home, at a distance of course, to the little house on Beauview Terrace. Once he was certain Celia's mother had spotted him but he took off quickly enough where she might have thought he had been at the neighbors'. Then he decided to write her a letter. He sent the first letter from the post box at the end of her street, then came back each day to watch the mail delivery until, finally, Celia came out to the box and found his letter. He watched her open it right there on the sidewalk and unfold it, reading his words as he watched.

He had written that they had met before but that was a lie. He said that only to make her more willing to correspond with him, thinking they had already been introduced, but after weeks of waiting there was no reply. And he had been smart too. Rather than writing his address on the envelope he had slipped in a calling card. Of course, Joel Sanders wasn't his real name and the address he gave belonged to a friend. Still, no matter how often he called that friend asking after the mail, there was nothing.

So he wrote again. And again. And again. Each time he watched her go to the box, and each time he saw her open the letter, read it, then tuck it back into the envelope. By then, any other man would have given up, moved on to another girl but for Joel there was no other girl, only Celia. Instead he began following her more often, closing the distance when he found her alone. He wrote and told her what he had seen, just to let her know he had been there, had seen her buying books, trying on dresses, having dinner.

When she went away to college he panicked. It took a little time and a little thought but he got his hands on a copy of her high school yearbook where there was a senior directory. There it was: College of Our Lady of the Elms, Chicopee. It wasn't a large campus but it was still difficult to track her down without being noticed. Men weren't allowed on campus and the girls were rarely allowed to leave on their own. For weeks he sat in his car, parked on Gaylord Street, waiting to catch a glimpse of her and it finally happened. She came out to see him and he couldn't have been happier.

Until she told him to leave. She said she didn't care that he was in love with her, that she had no idea who he was and had no interest in knowing. Her voice was getting louder and Joel worried that someone would hear or worse, see. He grabbed her and shook her a few times, hard, until she stopped talking. He ignored the fear in her eyes as he spun her around to the car, knocking her off balance. All it took was one shove and the back of her knees hit the frame of the car, buckling under her and sending her spilling onto the front seat like a ragdoll. Joel quickly grabbed her feet and shoved her the rest of the way, sliding in after her and pulling the door shut.

"Celia get up! I'm so sorry if I hurt you. You need to get up!"

He shook her leg, peering down into the dark, examining her face, tears streaming down her cheeks. Suddenly he heard the heavy slam of a door. His window was still open and he looked up to see a girl, a very tall blond, standing on the steps of the college watching him. He was too far away for her to see his face but he wasn't taking any chances. He threw the car in gear and mashed the pedal to the floor, taking off like a shot for the stop sign at the end of the street where he sailed through with barely a glance to the right and left. The car skidded around the corner and he yanked the wheel to keep from going off the road but it seemed he had over corrected sending the car sliding the other way where his front tire hopped the curb with a sickening thud.

Celia had managed to pull herself up into the passenger seat just as the tire caught the curb and she screamed. Joel righted the car just in time to see a second girl standing at the front doors watching him. He could see her face clearly and if he could see her, then she could see him. As he sped away, another girl appeared on the stairs and he thought perhaps they might chase after him but they didn't and by that point he was far enough away that he was likely in the clear. The two girls had already walked away, back to the building, but it scared him that the girl on the front steps had seen him and could describe him. He was distracted by the thought of the police coming for him and Celia took advantage of his divided attention, leaning over and yelling as Joel snapped back to reality and struggled to roll up his window before someone heard her.

"Lillian! Betty! Help me!" Joel reached out and slapped her hard on the cheek. She looked shocked for a moment, then angry. She launched herself at him, clawing at his face and neck, screaming like a banshee, threatening to run him off the road. Wrapping his fingers in her lustrous red hair Joel pulled her head back then smashed it against the steering wheel. He was surprised when she went limp under his hand and blood pooled on the leg of his pants. It looked like he had knocked her out.

He hadn't meant to hurt her like that but at least now she was quiet. Joel reached the junction at the end of Springfield Street, the one with the little island in front of Teta's auto shop, and swung around it onto Hampden Street, then cut all the way down to Center Street before finding himself on Front Street. Celia still wasn't moving, laying motionless on the front seat as Joel tried to figure out where to go now that he had a girl bleeding in his car. He hooked a left on Grove Street and found himself at the tire factory. Before he had time to talk himself out of it, he pulled up to the gate and got out, reached into his pocket for the key to the padlock, and opened it just far enough for him to drive in.

It had been almost a year since he had been fired from the factory but they had forgotten to ask for his keys back. Joel held onto them thinking that one day they might come in handy. Today was that day. He edged his car past the gate then got out to lock it behind him so no one would notice and come looking behind the building. With his headlights off so as not to attract attention, Joel made his way to the rear of the factory where the property was bordered by a brick wall and cut the engine.

Looking over at Celia, he watched the blood that was now drying on her upper lip, the bruise that was spreading across the bridge of her nose. There was no way she was going to forgive him for this, not after she had said all those things about hating him and wanting him to just go away. How could she say those things when she had read all his letters? She had to know they were meant to be together but not like this. Not when she was so clearly delusional. "She'll never forgive me," he whispered, brushing her hair back from her face and trailing his fingertips over her cheek.

He got out of the car and went around to the passenger side where he opened the door and reached in, grabbing both of Celia's arms so he could drag her out of the car. She was a lot heavier than he expected and it was difficult to drag her. It would have been easier if she was conscious and could walk but then if that was the case they wouldn't be in the situation they were now in. Joel shook his head, exasperated at Celia for making him do this. "It could have been so simple Celia." But she didn't reply. She couldn't hear him, not that he thought she would listen. Not now.

Instead he continued to drag her, her blazer catching on the thorny plants that dotted the landscape behind the factory, the heels of her shoes leaving visible tracks from the car. Joel would have to do something about those before he left but that would be an easy fix. Just use his own foot to scuff those marks out. No one would think twice. Not that anyone ever looked back here. You couldn't even see this part of the property from the building with its windows that were so high up you couldn't see out even if you were standing on your toes.

When Joel was satisfied he had found a good spot that was far enough from the edge of the building to be well protected, he sat Celia up against the brick retaining wall and took a moment to look at her, really look at her. He had been following her for so long, staring at her from the shadows, that it had been ages since he had just looked at her face. She looked so peaceful. If it wasn't for the blood Joel could imagine she was just taking a nap, perhaps on the couch next to him while they watched television. Her eyelids fluttered just then and Joel realized that if he was going to fix this thing he needed to do it now.

Grabbing her by either side of her head he pulled her forward, then quickly slammed her skull against the brick. He couldn't bear to look at her so he closed his eyes as he repeatedly smashed her head, breaking her into pieces. He finally stopped when he was sure she was no longer breathing and there was no chance that she could be revived. Laying her down against the wall, Joel went to work covering her with whatever debris he could find. The ground was heavy with the leaves the trees had shed coupled with the garbage that had found its way to this disused tract of land. It took a great deal of effort since he only had his hands to do it but Joel managed to cover her well enough that all it would take was a good cold snap, maybe even an early snowfall, and Celia Graves would never be found again.

It was a shame it had to end that way, Joel thought as he got back in his car and slowly backed up until he was at the gate again. He unlocked it, backed out, and closed and locked it behind him. When he was done it looked as if no one had been back there in ages. The final piece that Joel had to take care of was the journal.

And now, weeks later, after careful planning, Lillian Hanley was going to be the key to getting those pages that connected Joel to Celia.

"Hey there!" Joel came around the corner of O'Leary Hall to find Lillian waiting on the steps. He was careful to only ever make plans with her that were within walking distance so she never saw his car. He couldn't risk her recognizing it. It was stressful enough meeting her for the first time, wondering if she had seen his face that night when he caused such a commotion but he breathed a sigh of relief when she looked at him and smiled without a hint of recognition.

The night of the party was clear and cool, the campus draped in gold from the glow of the streetlamps that dotted the sidewalks. A small group of girls gathered on the steps to O'Leary Hall waiting for their dates, the door propped open so everyone could come and go as they pleased. Faint strains of music filtered out from the the windows that were all open just a crack to let in the fall air. Joel straightened his tie as he scanned the group on the steps searching for Lillian. He planned to escort her into the party, have a glass or two of punch, dance with her a bit, then beg off to use the restroom. With any luck, he'd have a clear path upstairs.

He spotted Lillian as she came through the door, craning her neck to see if Joel was there on time. She smiled when she saw him and raised her hand to wave. Joel waved back and started up the steps towards her where she stood, looking immaculate in her black dress with a tiny strand of pearls at her neck. For a brief second Joel imagined grabbing hold of those pearls and twisting them against her throat until the necklace broke. Instead he told her how lovely she looked.

"Thanks so much for inviting me. I hope I didn't put a crimp in your plans to ask some other dashing young man to be your date for real." Joel gave her a smile that he hoped came off as bright and carefree while inside he was anxious to get moving.

"Not at all!" Lillian said, returning his smile. "I'm glad we could do this together. It's going to be so much fun."

"Then shall we?" Linking his arm in hers, Lillian led Joel to the stairs that sank into the basement where the music streamed towards them, pulling them down to the party. There was a room tucked under the stairs that Joel never would have noticed if it wasn't for this party.

"Oh," Lillian breathed as they walked into the room. "Look at all the decorations! It looks completely different!"

"You've spent time down here before?" The lights were dimmed and streamers expertly strung, a massive crystal punch bowl sitting in the corner on a wooden table. In the opposite corner was a record player with a stack of records piled next to it. What little furniture there was in the room had been pushed to the side along with the billiards table which had been covered just in case someone might spill.

Lillian led Joel over to a group of girls and began introducing him around. He was immediately uncomfortable but tried not to show it. This was all part of the plan, acting like a normal date, escaping notice by blending in and going along with the evening. He grabbed two glasses of punch from the bowl and carried them carefully back to Lillian where a new group of girls and their dates had rotated into her orbit. Joel smiled at each one in turn as Lillian introduced them, then melted into the background while they all chatted. It was still early so no one was dancing yet which made Joel exceptionally impatient. He wanted to get his plan in motion as quickly as possible but he was at the mercy of the night.

Finally Lillian turned to him as the crowd around her dispersed and asked him if he was having fun. "Of course I am. This is great!" he lied.

"Good I'm glad. Would you like to dance? As head girl it's my responsibility to be the first out on the floor."

Perfect, Joel thought. *Time to get moving.* He held his hand out for Lillian and they swept out onto the dance floor, Lillian beaming at the other students as if she was royalty taking the stage at a coronation ball. Someone dropped the needle on a simple waltz and as the music swelled, other couples began stepping onto the floor with them. Joel looked around and realized that everything was going exactly to plan. Everyone was occupied including Lillian and all he had to do now was excuse himself to go to the restroom. With any luck, someone else would cut in and keep her occupied.

The song ended and Joel bent forward to excuse himself. "I need to use the restroom. Do you know where I would find one?"

Lillian pointed out to the foyer. "Just head upstairs and hang a right down the main hall. There's a restroom there."

"Thank you very much my lady!" Joel headed up the stairs and made like he was headed for the main hallway hoping no one could see him. He doubled back and took the stairs two at a time until he made it to the third floor. From there he was a bit less certain where he was going. Lillian had only said that Celia's room was tucked away in a corner, not easily seen from the main corridor. Joel was hesitant to waste time going up and down hallways searching for her room but it couldn't be helped.

Thankfully the first hallway was a dead end with no nooks or crannies branching off in either direction. The next hallway led to little more than a bathroom and a staircase so it had to be the final one. Joel ducked down the hallway, finding the alcove to his left and only one door-- it had to be Celia's. He jiggled the knob but it was locked. Thankfully he had expected as much and pulled a small lock picking kit from his back pocket. It was something that had been sold at the five and dime as a joke but it was made of rather sturdy metal and actually worked when he tested it on his bathroom door.

Kneeling down so he was eye level with the knob, Joel worked carefully to pop the lock. It took him longer than he had hoped but after a few moments he heard the satisfying click of the lock tumbling open. He stood and poked his head out of the alcove to make sure there was no one there. Reassured that the coast was clear, Joel opened the door and stepped quietly into Celia's room, closing the door behind him.

He thought back to that last conversation he had with Celia when she told him she had written everything about him in her journal. She had said it was hidden somewhere no one would ever find it but there were only so many places to hide something in a room without closets or corners. Joel walked the perimeter of the room but couldn't find anything obvious. No hidey holes in the plaster, no loose baseboards. On his second trip around the room he used his toe to tap the floorboards which yielded nothing until he found himself in front of the one and only window in the room where the boards sounded strangely hollow under his feet. Bending down, Joel used the heel of his hand to push on the end of one of each board until it started to give and flip up. He grabbed the loose end with his other hand and gently lifted the board up and out, revealing a neat little hiding place below. Sticking his hand into the darkness, Joel rooted around until he felt the edges of what had to be a book. He closed his fingers around it and pulled it from the hole.

Joel couldn't help himself. He stood up and started flipping through the book, looking for any mention of him. He got to the middle of the book and realized there were quite a few pages that Celia had dedicated to documenting his correspondence with her, all the times she noticed him following her, even his license plate number. She had recorded extremely accurate physical descriptions, listing what he was wearing each time she spotted him melting into the crowd. It was certainly damning.

There was quite a bit but it all seemed to be concentrated in the middle of the journal, sandwiched between regular everyday journal entries. He wondered if the police had already searched her room. Had they known about the journal and just not found it? Or had they not done a thorough search yet? Should he take the whole thing and risk rousing suspicion, or should he just take the pages that pointed the finger at him? In the end the decision was easy: there were footsteps coming down the hall, someone calling his name. *Lillian.*

Joel quickly ripped the pages from the journal and dropped it back into its hiding place. He was just replacing the floor board as the door opened and Lillian appeared behind him. "Joel? What the hell are you doing in here?"

Had she seen him replacing the floor board? Or worse, had she seen him with the book still in his hands? He knew he shouldn't have turned his back on the door; what a mistake that had been. Lillian was still standing in the doorway and Joel had balled the pages together and jammed them in his pocket where he brushed something metal-- the lockpicking kit. As Lillian continued to stare, Joel pushed the lock picking tweezers hard into the palm of his hand causing his eyes to fill. He looked up at Lillian and let the tiniest bit of moisture tumble down his cheek.

"I'm so sorry I disappeared on you. I just…" he sniffed for effect and swiped at the crocodile tear snaking its way to his chin. "I just wanted to be close to her one more time." He lifted his arms then let

183

them drop dramatically, making him look as dejected and heartbroken as possible. "I miss her so much."

"Oh you poor thing." Lillian sounded sympathetic but she didn't come any closer. She seemed hesitant to cross the threshold. "We should probably get back downstairs though before someone knows you've been up here."

Joel nodded miserably, shuffling out of the room looking suitably contrite. He pulled the door shut behind him but realized that he couldn't lock it behind him without a key.

"Wait a minute," Lillian looked down at the door handle. "How did you get in here? Her room has been locked since the police were here."

Shrugging, Joel began walking away, hoping Lillian would drop it and walk away with him. "It was unlocked. I just tried the knob. I guess I got lucky."

Lillian looked like she was having a hard time believing him but didn't quite know how to challenge him. "Well, I'll have to let the RA know it was open so they can lock it again."

Of course she would. And the moment she did that, they would know someone had been in there and if Lillian had come looking for him, he could be reasonably sure someone else in that dance knew she had left to find him. He realized in that moment that Lillian would have to go too.

CHAPTER NINETEEN

"So you got rid of her." Nora watched Joel's face change from placid and normal to twisted and enraged as he talked about both girls. Lillian's only crime was catching Joel in the act of stealing Celia's diary and for that, she had to die. As he told his story, he looked down at his shoes or up at the ceiling, depending on what part of the tale he was telling which meant he wasn't paying much attention to Nora who had slipped her hand in the pocket of her sweatpants where she had tucked her phone away, hidden by her robe. Her knees were bent to her chest and she was just able to see the screen of her phone without sliding it out too far. She hit the call button and hoped for the best.

"We had lunch the next day in the College Center. I slipped rat poison into her tea. She said it tasted funny but she drank it anyway." Joel reflexively tightened his grip on Selena as he spoke, his eyes once again finding Nora as she pulled her robe over her chest, hopefully concealing her phone completely. "We sat and talked for a little while– about the party, her friends, some of the things she had planned that week and then I offered to walk her back to her room."

It actually didn't take much rat poison to make a person sick– just 1.5 milligrams– but it was slow-acting. It normally took nearly two weeks for someone to feel the effects so Joel must have given Lillian quite a bit for her to feel sick so quickly. Yet Joel had also underestimated Lillian. He thought she would just go back to her room, fall asleep, and never wake up. Instead, she somehow found the strength to get up and go to class where the janitor would later find her, drawing even more attention to the circumstances of her death. Of course, he still got what he wanted when Lillian's parents chose to keep the poisoning quiet.

"They let a killer go free for almost sixty years." Nora studied the lines on Joel's face, the gray of his hair, the slight stoop of his shoulders despite the strength with which he was holding Selena. He had gotten to live an entire life after ending Lillian's and Celia's and here he was with his arm around Selena's shoulders, squeezing harder and harder as Selena winced in pain and fear. As Nora watched, helpless, Joel reached into his pocket and pulled out a knife, a small folding one with a sharp and pointy blade.

"Until you two came along." Joel flicked the blade open with a rather dramatic flick of his wrist. "Imagine my surprise when I'm watching the news in the maintenance office at the Elms and I hear my name."

The maintenance office? Nora made eye contact with Selena. He had been right there all along, right under their noses. And now they knew how he had managed to track them down. "You've been there the whole time?"

"I started working there right after Lillian. I wanted to keep an eye on that nun."

Sister Eleanor had been mere feet away from Lillian's killer and had no idea. When he hand delivered those threats to her he had done so from the basement of Berchman's. She was lucky he had never carried out any of his threats the way he had with Lillian and Celia.

"The only thing that saved her was that she didn't know who I was," Joel snickered, a sound that made Nora's skin crawl. "She walked by me nearly every day and most days she actually said hello to me!" He seemed delighted by this prospect, that Sister Eleanor coexisted with a murderer, was even kind to him from time to time.

As Joel continued to tell his story, Selena had gone suspiciously still. Nora tried not to look at her, maintaining eye contact with Joel, keeping his attention on her and not on Selena but she briefly caught Selena's eye and a nearly imperceptible lift of her chin. What on earth was she doing? Nora realized it didn't matter as she spied motion in front of the house. A cruiser had silently pulled up to the curb in front of the house next door and Dave slid from the driver's seat with another officer right behind him. They slowly approached Nora's front door, the tops of their heads barely visible as they crouched across the lawn. Nora wondered if there were more officers, perhaps circling the back of the house too. She held her breath as the screen door creaked open, hoping Joel wouldn't hear, but that was not the case.

"What was that?" Joel's head jerked in the direction of the front door, loosening his grip on Selena.

"What was what?" Nora asked, hoping to distract him from the doorknob that was slowly turning. Thankfully Joel hadn't thought to lock the door when he came in and slammed it behind him.

He never had a chance to answer. As he focused on the door, Selena took advantage of the opportunity to clamp down on his arm, biting hard until he cried out and bent forward. She drove her elbow into his stomach and dropped her weight until Joel let go of her to protect his stomach against a second blow. The moment he bent in half the door burst open and Dave flew at Joel, dragging him to the floor wrestling his arms behind him and cuffing him. The second officer followed close behind and was tending to Selena as Nora heard shouts coming from her backyard. So there had been reinforcements…

Dave checked the cuffs as he stood and headed for Nora. "Didn't I tell you not to find anything else before we could get here?"

"Ha ha. Very funny."

"Very smart, calling me from your cell."

"How much did you hear?"

"Enough to know we needed to get over here quickly." Dave glanced over his shoulder to make sure Joel was still on the floor. He was remarkably quiet now that he no longer had his hostage or his knife which had shot across the floor when Dave half-tackled him. "Are you okay?"

"Okay-ish," Nora replied, pointing to her knee. "I can't get up. It made a pretty terrible noise earlier."

Dave sighed and then spoke into the radio on his shoulder. "Send me an ambulance for a female with a knee injury."

The other officers came around the front of the house and loaded Joel into the back of a cruiser, whisking him away. Selena came over and sat next to Nora as they waited for the ambulance. They both knew better than to discuss what had just happened before giving their formal statements so they sat silently, Nora sinking into the throbbing that coursed through her knee as Selena sat with her chin in her hands, watching the front door that stood open in anticipation of the medics' arrival. This was going to be a fun one to explain to her orthopedic surgeon.

CHAPTER TWENTY

"It's hard to believe we ended up here because of an urban legend." Selena leaned back in her chair and put her pen down. There was still quite a line waiting to get their books signed but her fingers were beginning to cramp up and she occasionally forgot how to spell her own name. Nora had warned her that would happen but Selena had thought she was kidding. Now she knew better.

"Don't tell Eric but he was right. Elms was exactly what I needed to get back into the groove." Nora continued signing and piling the books at Selena's elbow for her to get to when she could feel her fingers again. "Who knew it was just a matter of giving Charley a partner in crime."

"What are you going to do with that other novel you wrote? The one Eric didn't want?"

Nora shrugged. "I'm not sure honestly. It's been sitting in a drawer for two years. Maybe it'll have its day in the sun but for now, my focus is our tour."

The first stop of which was the reading room on the second floor of Berchmans where Sister Eleanor was shaking hands while Nora and Selena were sequestered behind a table that groaned under the weight of over a hundred hardcover books. Already *Murder at the Alma Mater* had outsold every one of Nora's previous books. There had been so much coverage in the paper— both local and national– that the book had moved up the bestseller lists like lightning, making Nora Phillips and Selena Petersen household names. There was even talk of a made for TV movie about Celia Graves' and Lillian Hanley's murders. Nora and Selena had been asked to help adapt the screenplay.

In the end, the Catherine legend still floated around, a story that would forever be passed down from one generation to the next of Elms girls, and now boys. But these days it was whispered alongside the very true story of the two girls who had tragically crossed paths with the wrong boy. It became a cautionary tale of the consequences of carelessness. What had started as a whim, an indulgence to distract Nora from her disappointment, had turned out to be an incredible twist of fate.

As for Charlie Donahue, Nora found she wasn't done with her quite yet after all. She and Selena had already started tossing around ideas for strengthening Charley's partnership with her new pal Sabrina. Maybe it was even time for Charley and Sabrina to take the show on the road...

Author's Note
&
Acknowledgements

This book is, at its heart, a love letter to my alma mater. I attended the Elms first as an undergrad in 1998, then again as a graduate student in 2005, and returned as an adjunct professor in 2021. Though the campus has changed quite a bit since I was an undergrad (that science building did indeed get built), some of my best memories are on that campus.

Now, for those who might wonder if any of the characters in this book are real, the short answer is no, they are not. However, there are a number of people from the Elms Community who inspired me in my writing journey.

First, Dr. Jasmine Hall who taught Detective Fiction and who was one of my favorite professors. Much like Nora, I developed a love for Janet Evanovich's Stephanie Plum series in Dr. Hall's class after I read *One For the Money*. That class took my obsession with mysteries and expanded it in an entirely new direction that ultimately led to the creation of this novel.

When I was an undergrad Sister Kathleen Keating was still president and I spent a lot of time in her office (*not* because I was a trouble maker). Her secretary, Sandy Talbot, was always happy to see me and would sit and chat with me any time I stopped by, even long after I had graduated. She would never have slipped Nora confidential records but she would certainly have gotten a kick out of helping to solve a mystery!

In this book, Sister Eleanor is an amalgamation of some of my favorite nuns. When I started at the Elms, I took World Religions with the very real Sister Eleanor Dooley whose name I borrowed for this book. She and her (biological) sister, Sister Mary Dooley were fixtures on the Elms campus for many years. Sister Patty Hottin, another of my favorite human beings, also helped to inspire my fictional Sister Eleanor, lending some of her spunk, personality, and sense of humor.

And finally, Mike Smith, the Reference and Information Literacy Coordinator at Alumnae Library who very much inspired the characater of Michael Brown, has tolerated my endless parade of random Elms-related questioning over the course of writing this novel and provided me with numerous resources on the history of the college.

Despite my love of the Elms, there was a lot I didn't know about its early days, but Dr. Thomas Moriarty's history of the college was a wealth of information and photographs. I have also found a treasure trove of press photos on eBay, including one of the original library in Berchman's taken shortly after it was built and before there were even books on the shelves that set the scene for Nora and Selena's conversation at the balcony overlooking the Irish Cultural Center which is now located in West Springfield.

Over the course of my three years at the Elms I built friendships that have lasted the more than twenty years since I graduated. My freshman year roommate, Krister Brouker Botelho bears absolutely no resemblance to Nora's obnoxious roommate, though we did wear quite a groove into the *Titanic* VHS tapes Kristen brought with her. The second half of freshman year I got to room with Kimberly Weaver Mitchell who, along with Kimberly McMahon Pouliot, spent hours with me in the basement of O'Leary Hall listening to music and dancing to *NSYNC. Our Soph Show was indeed titled "The Wizard of Elmstock" and we dedicated it to our junior Big Sisters. Even though my Sophomore and Junior years were combined, making me something of an anomoly, I was very lucky to have Cristen Johnson as my Big Sister, helping me to adjust to living away from home for the first time and cramming four years of school into three.

Nora's roommate Margaret is an amalgamation of all the amazing, wonderful women I met while I was at the Elms: Valerie Opielowski Maldonado and her sister Catherine Opielowski Lawless, Jennifer Feldman Hamel, Nathalie Gagnon, Carissa Gibson Darm, and Celia Maldonado Rivera. Thank you all for making college the best years of my academic life!

And speaking of entertaining random questions, many thanks to Dan Outhuse for always being willing to consider bizarre hypothetical crime-related questions with only a moderate amount of mocking, and for providing the inspiration for Detective Dave Morris and his subtle snark.

I hope I did justice to my love for the Elms and my time there in this book and that many generations of Elms students enjoy this fictional romp through campus.

Printed in the USA
CPSIA information can be obtained
at www.ICGtesting.com
LVHW031537110324
774153LV00007B/608